THE NO-RETURN TRAIL

By the Same Author

★★★★★★★★★★★★

JASON AND THE MONEY TREE

JOURNEY TO AMERICA

THE MARK OF CONTE

ROANOKE: A Novel of the Lost Colony

RITA, THE WEEKEND RAT

A SINGLE SPECKLED EGG

WHO OWNS THE MOON?

BEYOND ANOTHER DOOR

Sonia Levitin

★★

THE
NO-RETURN
TRAIL

★★

New York and London

Harcourt Brace Jovanovich

Printed in the United States of America

Library of Congress Cataloging in Publication Data

Levitin, Sonia, 1934–
The no-return trail.

Bibliography: p.
SUMMARY: A fictionalized account of the 1841 Bidwell-Bartleson expedition which included seventeen-year-old Nancy Kelsey, the first American woman to journey from Missouri to California.
1. Kelsey, Nancy, 1823 or 4–1896—Juvenile fiction.
[1. Kelsey, Nancy, 1823 or 4–1896—Fiction.
2. Overland journeys to the Pacific—Fiction]   I. Title.
PZ7.L58No   [Fic]   77–88964
ISBN 0-15-257545-6

First edition

B C D E F G H I J

In memory of my teacher,

Walter Van Tilburg Clark,

who also loved the West

THE NO-RETURN TRAIL

1

★★

It was quiet now on the prairie—the deep, heavy quiet that
seemed to weight you down inside. Now and then Nancy
heard the distant moan of some wild creature. Then she would
turn toward the cradle and draw the baby nearer to her. There
were wolves. She had seen two of the gray prairie wolves
skulking around their camp that evening. She'd never actually
heard of wolves attacking people, but those glinting green eyes
were enough to make you shiver. They seemed like cowardly
varmints, waiting for some other creature to do the killing.

Nancy had begged Ben, "Let's not use the tent tonight!"
She needed to see the stars. The stars might comfort her.
Reluctantly Ben had agreed. Yes, she and the baby, Ann,
could sleep out, but under the wagon, mind, and not out in the
open. She could look at the stars from there, just so she stayed
down under cover and out of sight. They were deep into
Nebraska territory. Ben himself was standing night watch.

Unable to sleep, Nancy listened to the night sounds, the
distant croak-croaking of frogs, the sudden whinny of a horse
—maybe her own beautiful Lightning. Mostly she listened to
the steady, heavy thudding of her own heart. Strange words
went round and round in her mind. No-return. No-return.
No-return trail. Like the clacking of wagon wheels, over and
over, no-return trail.

They were only a month out, and already someone had
died. His name formed another endless pattern in Nancy's
mind. George Shotwell. No-return.

They had buried George Shotwell that afternoon. The Reverend Williams had given a long prayer, certain that George was a Methodist. Father De Smet, the Catholic priest, hadn't argued. Later Nancy saw him kneeling at the grave giving his own prayer for George Shotwell's soul.

The priest had seen Nancy sitting on a log nearby. "He is in God's hands now," Father De Smet had said, his face calm.

"He was really just a boy still," Nancy had mumbled, "no more'n eighteen." She had looked away to hide the turmoil of her feelings. She hadn't spoken directly to the priest before. His dark robes and the large cross were strange and somehow frightening.

Pleasantly the priest nodded. "Near your own age, Mrs. Kelsey. Even a short life can make one happy and proud. Our friend did set out to go west. He took a chance. Many men never do."

Nancy bit her lip. "His ma was against his coming," she said. Then she sat silently, staring down at the scrubby growth of weeds and an ugly lizard, which showed its head out from a rock.

When Nancy looked up again, the priest was gone, and for the first time she had allowed herself to cry. Only a few tears came. The rest she pushed back, clenching her fists, forcing herself to swallow again and again.

"The trail," she told herself sternly, "is no place for tears."

They were her pa's words, suddenly clear and loud as when Pa had said them, when she was little and they'd moved from Kentucky to Missouri. She'd gotten her toe nearly mashed when one of the wagon wheels slipped and ran over her foot. She had screamed in pain. An hour later she still whimpered, for she was only three years old.

Pa had ridden up alongside the wagon, where he'd allowed her to sit just this once. "It's near time to stop for nooning," he had told her. "We'll stop by the river, and you'll go soak your toe in the water. And then, Nancy, I don't want to hear another word about your toe. You whine, and I'll whip you. The trail," he said, "is no place for tears."

Nancy had learned not to cry. Now she lay very still, staring up at the stars, bright and brittle as icicles. She wondered whether she'd ever learn not to feel the sorrow. Her whole body ached with the weight of it.

Ben, before leaving for guard duty, had touched her hand briefly. He had said, with some surprise, "Why you grieving so? He was a stranger to us."

Nancy had not replied. Instead, she had busied herself cleaning the pan with sand from the riverbank. It was best not to talk about some things.

True, George Shotwell was a stranger to them. But Nancy felt a kinship, for he, too, was born in Kentucky. George had never talked much, either. Nancy felt a kinship with his silence. It came from living in the woods. It went along with the toughness only home-folks had. Toughness that made it possible for a man to take his ax and hack off his own left hand when it was mangled in a bear trap. Nancy had heard tell of this when she was only six and gone to town with her pa. She had seen the man's stumpy arm to prove it.

George Shotwell, for all his slender build, was the kind who wouldn't run from anything. Nancy knew that because she knew Kentucky folks. Except that she'd never before known anyone who shot himself.

"Damn fool!" some of the men had shouted, astonished and angry. "Damn fool, doesn't he know how to get out of a wagon? Goes and shoots himself?"

Of course, they'd thought he would live, that the accident would be just another story to tell around the campfires. All their lives when talk got to wagon trains and accidents they'd tell it, sucking on their pipes, sipping hot coffee.

"I remember in our wagon train a young fella from Kaintuck, allus in a hurry, got out his wagon one mornin', shot hisself plumb through the belly. Guess he's still carrying that lead in his gut, guess he's learnt himself a lesson about carryin' a gun."

They had all thought he would live. Their guide, Captain Fitzpatrick, gave him some medicine from a small vial. The stopper was gummy with dirt. Still, Fitzpatrick uncorked it and poured a good bit into George Shotwell's mouth, muttering, "Laudanum—it'll do him."

But George had sunk into fever, until he was fiery red and soaked with sweat and clear out of his head. "Mama!" he kept calling. "I didn't go swimmin', Ma, like you told me. Here I am, Ma! I didn't go in the water."

Fitzpatrick had come for Nancy. "Can you do anything for him, ma'am?" He removed the plug of tobacco from his mouth and placed it in his pocket. "You've got a way with curing horses," he said hopefully. "We thought maybe you'd have something. . . ."

Nancy had reached inside her cloth satchel, knowing all the while that she had nothing but herbs and mineral oil, salts and liniment—nothing to cure a dying man.

"Mind the baby!" she told Ben. She ran to the shade of a wagon where George Shotwell lay, his head propped up on a log.

Gently Nancy had lifted his head, motioning the men to remove the log. With a cloth soaked in a mixture of spring water and salts, she first cleaned the wound, then wiped his head again and again.

"Ma!" he screamed out once. Then he was dead.

Now he lay buried in the wilderness near a place called Ash Creek. Ben had said they'd auction off his things when they got to Fort Laramie. Everything that had ever meant anything to George Shotwell would be traded away. His bones would soon be scattered upon the prairie, for there were the wild creatures, and they were hungry.

Again and again now the words repeated themselves in Nancy's mind, like a song. No-return trail. She wondered, where did songs come from? Who made them up? Did you have to be able to write them down? If she ever made up a song, she thought, it would likely be a sad song. A song about partings. A song about going west and dying.

But she had wanted to go west. Hadn't she? She herself had railed and stormed about coming. She had wanted to go to California. Hadn't she?

Nancy closed her eyes tightly, trying to remember. She could not. As hard as she tried, she couldn't remember Ben ever actually asking her or talking it over.

"Guess I'd like to join that wagon train to Californ-y," Ben had said. "We could get ourselves a good spread."

She had only stared at him dumbly. What had she thought then? What had she *wanted?* She lay very still under the stars, wakeful, trying to remember.

2

★★

Ben had said, "Guess I'd like to join that wagon train to Californ-y. We could get ourselves a good spread."

Nancy had stared at him dumbly. Her hands moved instinctively to her stomach.

"My brothers are thinkin' of going, too," Ben had said. "Sam's gonna bring Sadie and the boys. Sadie thinks maybe the men should go ahead first and get settled."

Nancy had said nothing, thinking only of the baby she carried in her belly. Not Ann then—not a real person yet—just "the baby." That was back in November. By the time the baby came, in February, Ben and his brothers might forget all about going west.

But they didn't forget. In February, when Ann was born, for a few weeks all talk of going west stopped. Then, gradually, it picked up again. Andy, Isaac, or Sam would drop by. Talk would turn, always, to going west. Yet Nancy and Ben did not really discuss it. Like a living thing, like creeping moss, the idea just grew.

Then came a day in April, and Nancy seemed to know beforetime that this was the day for settling it. It wasn't the first time she'd had such a notion. She'd known the very day Ben was going to ask her to marry him; she'd known beforetime the day her pa died.

That April evening Nancy rebraided her hair and put on a clean apron. She threw another log onto the fire and watched as the sparks leapt up. Immediately a warm glow filled the cabin, giving a flush of color to the mud-chinked walls.

☆ **8** ☆

She moved Ann's little makeshift bed closer to the fire. For a few minutes she sat down, rocking gently in her chair. She'd washed down the floor this morning. Everything was in its place, the table cleared, the dishes stacked neatly on the shelves. Now, she thought with a slight sigh, if only the baby would be good.

Ben, in from tending the animals, stood for a moment at the open door, calling, "You want the cat inside?"

"Heavens, no!" She rushed toward him. "And take your boots off. You know how Sadie gets, remarking on every speck of dirt."

"Come on, Nancy, don't fuss. Sam doesn't come over that often."

"Who'd ever fuss at Sam?" Nancy asked, astonished. "It's Sadie always finds fault, at least where I'm concerned."

"Maybe you're too thin-skinned," Ben remarked, and Nancy bit her lip at the reproach. A moment later Ben's arms were around her, and he whispered against the side of her neck, "Just Sam and me are going to talk. Probably Sadie won't come anyhow. Don't be cross."

"She treats me like a child!" Nancy burst out.

"Sadie's always been bossy," Ben said softly. "*I* know you're a grown woman," he said, grinning. "Now, please, if she does come . . ."

In that moment they heard the clatter of the cart, and Nancy knew Sadie had come too. Otherwise Sam would simply have ridden the three miles on horseback.

Ben threw open the door. "Sadie! Glad you could make it. The boys okay? Come on in. Nancy'll fix us some coffee. Hey, Sam, I was thinking I ought to try and buy a new rifle, or at least get this one fixed. Look here . . ."

By and by the men had settled down to talk by the fire. Nancy washed up the coffee mugs. Then she and Sadie sat at the table talking while Nancy worked on her hooked rug. It was pleasant and easy, and nothing out of the way was said. Sadie even remarked, "Pretty colors there, Nancy. I've neglected my own stitching." She sighed. "Seems like every night I'm still baking or cleaning."

For the first time it occurred to Nancy how tired Sadie must be with five little boys to take care of, and them bringing in all sorts of stray animals all the time.

"The boys found any critters lately?" Nancy asked, making a tight loop.

"Just a dead rat," Sadie said with a grimace.

There was an easy silence between them, while Ben and Sam talked on in their rumbling voices. "Hear it gets mighty wet on the trail . . . rubberized sheets on the ground . . . think they sell nails in California?"

Nancy only half listened to the talk. It was warm in the cabin, and her eyes felt heavy, while the talk soothed her like a song.

Suddenly Sadie's voice broke through, loud and angry. "If you ask me, Ben, it's downright foolishness for you even to think of taking Nancy and . . ."

"Aw now, Sadie," Sam began mildly.

"No, Sam!" She rose up angrily, scraping her chair. "I aim to speak up when I see my own kin acting like they've gone plumb crazy! It's crazy for a woman to go tramping across the country, and her no more'n seventeen and carrying a baby!"

"But your sister, Lindy . . ." Ben broke in.

"How can you compare, Ben Kelsey?" Sadie exclaimed. Her pale blue eyes widened, and her moon-round face, usually so pale, began to flush with her vehemence. "My sister Lindy is twenty years old, and *her* child is four. Little Mary can walk. Mary don't have to be *carried!* But taking an infant, Holy God, you'd think Nancy herself would see . . ."

"Don't you talk blasphemy, Sadie!" Sam shouted, and Nancy almost smiled despite her rising anger. Sam, old Sam could cuss the stopper right out of a whiskey flask, as Andy and Isaac always said. But Sam didn't hold with letting a woman use the Lord's name in vain.

"Nobody said you shouldn't go, Ben," Sadie continued, her

tone softer, almost wheedling. "It makes sense for you to come ahead with us, and then send for Nancy when we get settled. By then Ann will be older. She'll be walking. Listen, I know what it's like when babies sicken." Her voice took on that high pitch. "I know, and I'm not just talking, having lost two of my . . ."

In that instant Nancy burst upon them, her heart racing. If she allowed Sadie a moment more in which to speak the names of her own two dead babies, all might be lost.

"Sadie!" She spat out the name, nearly shouting. "I'm married to Ben, and I aim to stick with him no matter where he goes! I'll do no such thing as sit here in this cabin and worry myself to death while you all go roaming around the countryside, what with the desert and Injuns and the Lord knows what else. . . . Don't you tell me what to do, Sadie Kelsey! Don't you dare!"

For a long moment there was dead silence as Sadie, Sam, and Ben stared at Nancy, astounded by her outburst. The fire gave out a single sharp crack.

"It's a hard trail, I hear tell," murmured Sadie, her voice lapsed into a sing-song. "You think you know about it, but I read about it in the paper. . . ."

Nancy's breath came in sharp gasps as she struggled to remain silent. How like Sadie to bring up the fact that she could read the paper! Next she'd remind them all that she'd taught school one winter for a few weeks, when the regular teacher was sick. Inwardly Nancy raged—Sadie and her airs!

"Yes, I read about some men from the East, went west for hunting. Oh, it's a hard, hard trail."

"Well, I like to think I can stand that 'hard, hard trail' as well as anybody!" Nancy clenched her fists inside the pockets of her apron. "I'm strong. You said yourself, after Ann was born, how you never saw a woman stronger, getting up the very next afternoon to help Ben bring in the ox. . . ."

Sam nodded. "Sadie, you did say it."

Sadie blew out her breath through pursed lips, slowly. "It's no matter to me a'tall," she said, shaking her head. "You always do what you've a mind to, Nancy Kelsey, never listening to anybody."

Suddenly Ann began to wail. To Nancy's humiliation, she couldn't quiet the baby. Sadie, watching, pursed her lips so tight that her cheeks seemed to bulge out.

At last Sadie walked over and wordlessly took the baby from Nancy. With a brisk motion she laid Ann over her knee. She gave the baby a smack on the back, turned her over and then back again. A loud, rolling belch came from the small baby, and Nancy only stared.

"There's lots to learn about babies," Sadie said briskly. "It's different helping take care of little brothers and sisters or tending your own. My sister Lindy doesn't mind a helpful hint now and then. But some people never want to take advice."

"Now, Sadie." Sam stood up, looking embarrassed. "We'd best head home."

Nancy held in her retort as long as she could. The moment Sam and Sadie were out the door, she let it come rushing out at Ben. "She just wants me to stay home so her sister Lindy can get her hands on you! Been widowed barely six months, and already she's runnin' after every man in the county! I knew Sadie would start trouble."

"It sure took you to finish it!" Ben snapped angrily. "I was ashamed."

"Why?" Nancy shouted. " 'Cause I want to go with you?"

" 'Cause you got no manners. They were our company."

Words followed words, hot and angry. At last they lay in bed, stiff and silent. Long after Ben had fallen fast asleep, Nancy kept thinking of better and sharper things she should have said. Angrily she planned that in California they'd get themselves a big spread. They'd live far, far away—maybe a few days' ride away—from anyone else named Kelsey.

3

★★★

The next morning there was a careful silence between Nancy and Ben. During the fight the night before she had declared that she planned to leave the next morning to go to her mother's house. In a way, telling Ma was like starting on the first leg of the trek to California.

Nancy cleared away Ben's dish, stopping near him for a moment longer than necessary. Let him end it, she thought. Let him sweet-talk her back into a good humor.

He only half turned toward her. "You leaving now?"

"Soon as I sweep up."

"You going to be all right?"

"Yes. There's cold pork and biscuits for your supper. I'll be back afternoon tomorrow."

She fed Ann, then bundled her in a shawl and wrapped her again in an old bearskin. Then she saddled up Lightning and set out.

In the early morning the wind was still biting cold. Nancy hadn't been out to go this far since Ann was born. It was about half a day's ride to Ma's place. Strange, now that she had the baby, things seemed different. The way seemed longer. Her back began to ache from the tension of holding the baby in her left arm and reining with her right. She dared not think how it might be on the trail, day after day.

Lightning kept a good, steady pace. He was a brown and white pinto, half quarter horse, half Indian pony, a racer in his youth. Nancy had never had a horse so keen. Her touch on the reins, the slightest whisper of her heel laid against his side, and he responded as if he could read her mind.

She rode across wide, empty fields, up and down gentle, rolling hills. Now and then a creek or a stream marked the way, or a homesteader's cabin, and Nancy ticked off the landmarks to herself—that clump of oaks, next old Henderson's place . . .

From behind a mass of boulders suddenly came a sharp, snapping sound. Nancy's hair seemed to rise on her scalp, and a shiver ran down the back of her neck. She clutched Ann more tightly, simultaneously feeling for the knife that lay concealed under her saddle.

Foul redskins! Anger overcame fear. Sometimes they'd sneak up even into civilized towns, raiding and killing. They'd lie in wait for travelers on the roads. Good sport for them to make a little baby and its mother die. Well, she had her knife. She'd use it! She fought the urge to spur Lightning ahead, but sat straight in the saddle, knowing that she did right, for one must never run from Indians, never.

Lightning knew. He moved steadily with a high, determined gait, every muscle taut. The next moment Nancy laughed aloud with relief as a harmless porcupine scurried away before her path.

"Lightning, you and me are getting skittish!" she said, still chuckling. "I think you're every bit as scared of Injuns and rattlesnakes as I am. Did I teach it to you, or were you that way on your own?"

Strange to see, the horse's head bobbed up and down, as if he were agreeing to whatever his mistress had said, and Nancy patted his neck, inhaling deeply that scent of him, sweat and flesh and hide. She could never understand how some folks didn't tolerate the smell of horses.

Nancy had put two johnnycakes and a handful of currants into her saddlebag. She'd planned to stop a spell and eat. Now she felt an urgency and decided to continue. Ann was asleep, but she was wet, and briefly Nancy wondered—how would she manage Ann's breechcloths on the trail?

They got to Ma's place early afternoon, but there were chores to do, some of them waiting for an extra pair of hands, and Nancy was glad to help. Then all the kids wanted to show Nancy their new treasures and tell her about how they'd grown to do new things since they last saw her, and of course they all had to see the baby.

When at last the kids were bedded down in the loft, Nancy and Ma sat beside the fire, mending together the way they used to do. Ann lay in the cradle at Nancy's feet, the same cradle she herself had lain in.

"Pa would like to know your own child was using it," Ma said. Then she added, "You keep it for Ann."

It was a good way to begin, Nancy thought. She said, "Thank you, Ma." Then she added, "I think Pa would be proud to have that cradle move on west."

Her mother looked up swiftly, her hands suddenly stilled. "West? You and Ben thinking of moving on?"

"We've been talking."

"Well, there's some good land to be had a bit closer to the river, but . . ."

"Ma, we wasn't thinking of just moving up-river," Nancy said.

"Oh? Where then? All west of the river is Indian territory, isn't it still?" she said smartly, pursing her lips. "Or have I missed something, Nancy Kelsey?"

"Yes. It's Indian country," Nancy said, swallowing hard. She gave the cradle a nudge with her foot. Maybe she and Ben should have talked to Ma together. Ben could make it all sound so reasonable and right.

In the silence Ma's rocker squeaked harshly, like the wheeze of an ailing man. Ma's eyes were fastened on her sewing, as if attention to her work would end the talk, make everything all right.

Nancy rambled on, uncertainly, repeating what she'd heard Ben say. "It's getting so crowded here, Ma. You remember how you always said Pa decided to leave Kentucky when neighbors moved close enough to hear his rifle shot? Well, you know how it is here. Game's going to run out, too."

"Oh?" said her ma. "Game's all gone? Wonder then what it was we had tonight in my pot pie. Seems to me there was a spot of meat." She bit off her thread, hard.

"You know what I mean, Ma." Her ma's eyes were again severely focused on her sewing.

"Ben says there's places out west—I mean, places like you never heard of. California, it's called. California." Nancy loved the sound of the name. It sounded like great herds of wild horses, cool breezes all summer, strawberries for supper, and no ugly varmints to pounce on people when they went for water, no murdering Injuns, never any misery at all.

"Ma, you know what I mean," Nancy said again. "People in California, why, they never get fever. Never, never have they had the ague."

Her mother's back stiffened at the word "ague."

"Ma! In California oranges grow on trees! The land's so rich, why, if you poke in a fence post, it'll sprout leaves in a week! The people—Ma, the people are so friendly. You can go anywhere without having to pay 'cause they love to have company. They'll let you stay for weeks and weeks, and give you a horse to get on your way."

Her mother said nothing, but the rocker creaked on, like a wheezing voice saying, "Silly. Silly. Silly."

"Ma," Nancy cried, wishing her mother would look at her. "Just last week Ben killed eighteen snakes out back of our cabin. The mosquitoes are eating us alive. Poor Ann's little cheek was all bit. We roast in summer, and in winter we freeze. In California it's always warm. What'll grow here? We'd like to have a garden, maybe even with flowers."

"No flowers in Missouri, I guess," her mother said tartly.

Carefully she laid her sewing into the basket. Slowly she turned the rocker to face her daughter. Then she began.

"Now, *you* listen, Nancy Kelsey, because I know all what you're saying. Further, I know exactly what you're going to say next. You're going to rattle on for miles telling me that California is heaven and that you and Ben and all his crazy brothers are going to go and live like angels in this paradise called Californ-y. Well, there is *no road* to California! Nobody's ever been there, but a few drunken mountain men, and I'd trust *their* word as far as I could throw a bear. Most likely there ain't even no place *like* Californ-y, but somebody just *invented* it. But beyond that, I happen to know what it's really like out there. Redskins, more than in Kansas. Wilder, too. Scalp you quick as anyplace. The Californios—a mean bunch of varmints. They'll string up a man quicker'n learn his name. Just last fall they strung one up. Poor beggar just visitin' from the east. Strung him up to a tree just like . . ."

Suddenly Ma stopped dead in the middle of her sentence. She moved the chair back, picked up her sewing, and began to stitch. Then softly she asked, "When you figuring on leaving, gal?"

"Why, as soon as the prairie's green," Nancy whispered. "Beginning of May, I reckon. We're supposed to meet a whole lot of other people in Sapling Grove. We'll all go west together. It'll be a big wagon train. About five hundred people, I guess."

Ma nodded. "Won't be any five hundred," she said. "Oh, I know a lot of folks *said* they're going to California. Got the bee in their bonnets way back last winter when that Frenchman with the fancy name told everybody how good it was out west."

Nancy only listened, awed. She never could figure how her ma knew everything. Mention a name to her, she'd heard it before. Talk about doings somewhere in the next county, and she'd know, all right. If folks in Missouri weren't so civilized, Nancy guessed they'd like to have called her a witch.

Nancy said, "Ben went to meetings at the schoolhouse and heard this Mr. Robideaux. Lots of folks agreed to get provisions for the trip. It's like you said. Sam and Isaac and Andy are going, too. Sam's bringing Sadie and the kids, and Lindy Gray is going. . . ."

Ma tossed her head. "So, the widow Lindy Gray can't find herself a man here in town, but she has to go find one on the trail!"

"The Kelseys is all the kin she's got," Nancy argued. "I expect it's best for her to go."

Again the rocker creaked its accusing refrain, "Silly. Silly. Silly." Then Ma rose and went to the sideboard that Pa had made years ago. It was fine and smooth, made of oak, by far the finest thing in the cabin. From the shelf Nancy's mother took a quilt.

"I've been saving this," she said, her face stiff, almost stern. "I started it a long time ago. I figured to give it to you for your wedding. I didn't get it done in time."

"But, Ma, you gave me the pewter jug and the rocker . . ."

"When I heard all this talk about a wagon train heading west, I knew right well you and Ben would be with it. I knew. So you take this here quilt, Nancy, and you take good care of that baby. Now, we'd best be off to bed. I've got baking to do in the morning, and a mess of wash. Let me hold my granddaughter a while."

Astonished that her mother would disturb the sleeping baby, Nancy watched silently. Baby Ann didn't even wake up when her grandmother gathered her into her arms and held her, rocking gently. It seemed a long time that Ma sat with the baby.

At last, from the bed in the corner of the cabin, Nancy watched Ma bank the fire and dim the lantern. It was strange to be sleeping in her mother's house again. It felt good not to be the one to draw in the latchstring and put up the bar, not to be the last in bed.

"Ma," Nancy whispered, "thank you for the quilt. I'm going to miss you. I—we'll come back to visit."

"Nancy."

"We will! You'll see. Ma, I want to tell you . . ." Words wouldn't come, at least not the right words. "I'll take good care of this quilt. I'll give it to Ann on her wedding day."

"Like as not," Ma remarked tartly, "by the time you get to California you'll be carrying two babies. Now you take care, Nancy, and say your prayers every Sunday." Softly she added, almost to herself, "Pray you don't get too many young'uns too soon. Babies is the Lord's blessing. But not when they come too fast."

Nancy grinned to herself in the darkness. "Guess you'd best talk to the good Lord *and* Ben Kelsey about that, Ma!"

"Look who's getting foul-mouthed and sassy! Lord, what a gal I've raised me." But she laughed all the same, and she was simpering still when she got down under the covers beside Nancy. In the next moment, or so it seemed, they were both sound asleep.

4

★★★

That was the last time Nancy saw Ma. What with tending the kids and the homestead, her mother seldom had time to visit. As for Nancy, the next weeks were the busiest of her life.

With the money Ben made from selling their cabin, he bought another ox, along with their staples—flour, salt, sugar, coffee, dried beans. It was Nancy's job to see to their clothes, to make extra soap and candles for the trail, to put up as many preserves as she could, and to get the new ox to working with its partner. An untrained animal on the trail could mean disaster.

While she worked with the ox, Nancy left the baby in a hammock slung between two trees. Over and over again she had to remind herself that oxen are poor, dumb animals. She had to fight to keep her temper, to keep herself from using the hickory switch. Instead, she let out her impatience by slapping viciously at the mosquitoes that lit on her arms and neck. She kept calm with the oxen. At last she could tell Ben, eyes glowing, but her features steady to conceal her pride, "I guess you can start using them together now, Ben."

Ben watched the team for a time as Nancy prodded gently with the hickory switch, murmuring, "Gee, Buck! Ho, Bright!" Then he said, "You'd think they'd been matched for years."

Warm with happiness, Nancy went to get the baby from her hammock. For a time the three of them stood in the field, gazing out over their small claim. Then Ben took Ann, and he put his other arm around Nancy's waist. Never had she felt happier, more peaceful, than at this moment.

At first, when Ben told her he'd gotten twenty-three whole dollars for the cabin, Nancy could hardly believe it.

"Ben!" She laughed and stared at the money. "I've never seen that much cash in my life! What'll we do with it all?"

"We'll buy you half a dozen bonnets," Ben said teasingly, "and a whole bolt of paisley silk."

"Ben Kelsey, you know perfectly well we'll need every penny of this money for food and tools." She dared not look at him. He would see her longing.

"Oh, I expect we'll have some left over for extras."

"Extras?" Nancy's breathing came fast and unsteady.

"I guess we could afford a few yards of a certain brown material I've seen a certain lady lookin' at whenever we go to town," Ben said, and Nancy knew he was proud of the trade he'd made, and very happy.

"That brown linsey-woolsey!" she exclaimed. "Oh, Ben, I do need a new shawl so bad, and there'd be enough left over for a wrapper for Ann!"

They went to Weston to the general store, and along with the linsey-woolsey, Ben insisted on buying Nancy a new bonnet.

"You wouldn't want to feel poor in front of all the other women, now, would you?"

"Will there be lots of other women, Ben?"

"Of course! Why, I expect you'll all be settin' around gossiping at night, worse than city folks," he said, grinning.

They bought a tan bonnet with a pale-blue lining. "It goes with your eyes," Ben said, and laden with packages, they left the store.

Outside, Nancy could hear a sudden burst of laughter. It held only scorn. "Some folks are never . . ." she heard them saying from inside, and she froze in her tracks. "See that little baby? Quicksand on the prairie . . . crazy folks . . . never satisfied . . . you could give me a hundred dollars and I wouldn't take . . ."

"Don't pay them any mind," Ben muttered. "Those shop-keepers just don't want us to move. They don't want to lose all their customers."

"Are really *that* many people going, Ben?" He made it sound as if there'd be nobody left in the whole country!

"A few hundred, I'd say," Ben said confidently. "We'll have plenty of company."

"Ben . . ." Nancy hesitated, reluctant to spoil this afternoon, with Ben so happy, but she had to ask it. "Ben, does anybody know how to *get* to California?"

"Now, Nancy, with all those folks planning all winter, don't you think they'd know the way? I know for a fact that one man has a map, and another has a letter from a friend in California, telling exactly how to get there. Nancy, there's some smart people going. One of 'em's a schoolteacher, name of Bidwell. I met him. He's traveled all over."

"Has he been to California?"

"Of course not, Nancy. Nobody's been to California."

They laughed nearly all the way home in the buckboard, singing out into the empty fields, "Nobody's been to California!"

Ben threw back his head and sang a song:

> "Haven't got a nickel
> And we haven't got a dime,
> But we're off to Californ-y
> Any old time!"

Nancy sang out with him. Then soberly she asked, "Is it true, Ben? Is the money all gone?"

"Nearly. We've got a little left for some extra horseshoes and ox shoes. Oh, and I forgot pickles."

"What on earth for? We don't even like pickles."

"Keeps you from getting sick on the trail," Ben said.

Silently, Nancy nodded. Ben seemed to know everything.

Men were like that, she thought wonderingly. They found out things. They even could make up songs *just like that.*

It was their last ride in the buckboard. Ben traded it, along with three dollars cash, for a wagon from a distant neighbor, Jenkins. Mr. Jenkins's wife had died in childbirth, along with their infant son.

"I'm going home to Boston," the man said sorrowfully. "Strange—you folks headed west in my wagon, me going east. River traffic's getting to be terrible. Well, good luck."

The wagon was small and needed fixing. Ben mended two of the wheels, while Nancy patched the cover. It was almost impossible to pull the needle through the tough canvas. Then, with Sam's help, Ben fitted new bows to the wagon.

Sam brought along his three oldest boys, aged ten, nine, and six. Six-year-old Luke was Nancy's favorite, though she tried to hide it. They raced through the cabin, chattering and asking a thousand questions, and even Nancy's sugar cookies couldn't quiet them for long.

"Aunt Nancy, don't you wish Uncle Ben would buy you a cow?"

"Sure do." Nancy ladled hot soap into pans. "But we can't afford a cow."

"But you got milk for the baby yourself, ain't you, Aunt Nancy," said Luke, his large eyes innocent, and Nancy smiled to herself. If Sadie were here, she'd whip him for talking so personal.

"Ann will be fine," Nancy said, nodding.

"You gonna have her ride in the wagon, Aunt Nancy?" asked Jeremy, the oldest.

"Oh, no, honey. I'd never do that. She might fall out and get killed."

"Then you gonna carry her all the way to California?"

Nancy chuckled slightly. "Lightning will carry her—and me."

"It's hard to ride and hold somethin'," said Billy solemnly.

Nancy sighed. She wished the boys wouldn't ask so many

questions. But long after they had left, those same questions still rang in her head. She thrust them aside. She guessed she'd figure things out once they were underway. For now, she had to concentrate on getting everything packed into that one small wagon. Nearly every inch of space was taken up with supplies. The large barrels were fastened down tight onto the false bottom Ben had built.

"What's that for, Ben?"

"You'll find out," Ben said brusquely.

"Ben, did you sell the table and chairs, too?" She glanced at the rough hewn straight chairs and the table Ben had made.

"Yes. You've asked that a dozen times, Nancy. You know they wouldn't fit into the wagon. I'll make new ones for you when we get to California."

When we get to California—everything centered on those words. It got so that Nancy couldn't wait to start. Then came the day of leaving, and there was this queer feeling in her stomach.

She looked around the small cabin. For a moment she could almost hear the neighbors and Ben's brothers laughing and shouting on that day they'd come to help raise the roof. She remembered how Isaac had yelled out, loud enough for the whole world to hear, "You'd better make a good-sized loft up there, Ben! You'll be bedding down a whole passel of young-'uns before you know it!"

Nancy gazed at the bed built into the corner, at the four-shelf cupboard Ben had made, at the two neat, small windows. They'd planned to get real glass for them someday.

"You ready?" Ben called to her from the door. "We want to get an early start. Sadie and Sam'll be meeting us on the road."

"Ben, that man who bought the cabin—did he really like it?"

"Nancy, we've got to get going!"

"Remember how I picked out those stones for the hearth? Remember how we hunted for them?"

"I remember," Ben said. He nodded impatiently.

They closed the door, but didn't lock it. The new owner would be there by nightfall. And by nightfall Nancy, Ann, Ben, and the other Kelseys would already have joined the other members of the Western Emigration Society. They'd be gathered and waiting at Sapling Grove, the rendezvous.

"Rendezvous . . ." Nancy turned the word over and over in her mind. She had heard Ben and Isaac using it. It had a nice sound, she thought. It seemed to go with the spots of sunlight sprinkling down through the trees. It semed to match Lightning's gait. She tried to rhyme it. *Rendezvous. Rabbit stew.*

Nancy glanced back over her shoulder, embarrassed at her own silliness. But there was nobody to pay her mind, except Ann. The baby was awake, bouncing gently in the sling Nancy had fashioned from an old shawl. With the ends of the shawl tied around Nancy's neck, Ann was held securely, but gently enough to be rocked by the motion of the horse. It felt good to have her baby so near, so warm. She bent her head and kissed the soft, smooth face.

Again Nancy looked back, imagining Sadie's face looking flat and hard with disapproval. Sadie did not believe in spoiling babies by kissing and such. But of course, she could not have seen. Through the thick, rising dust Nancy could see only the vague forms of wagons and beasts, heaving and swaying together, moving laboriously as if they had been straining onward forever.

Sam's wagon, the largest of the three, was crammed so full that you couldn't get a bedbug to fit. Behind Lindy's smaller wagon came the three pack mules belonging to Andy and Isaac. They had promised to help Lindy with her team, in exchange for storing some of the staples in her wagon. Sadie rode in the cart with her two youngest boys. All together they spread out into a straggling, untidy caravan.

Ahead, Nancy could see the faint trail of dust left by Isaac's horse. She urged Lightning into a gentle lope, to catch up.

As Nancy approached, Isaac slowed his horse and turned to

grin at her, glad for company. Though Andy was the young-est, Isaac seemed the most boyish. He smiled the most.

"Should be just ahead over this rise," he said. "They told us to look for a stand of young hickory trees by a creek."

"You want to slow down so we can all ride in together?"

"Good idea."

Nancy envisioned their small wagon train riding into the clearing. She was glad for the size of Sadie's wagon. It was impressive. A real mattress with springs could be seen sticking out the back. Folks would look up when they heard them all rolling into camp. No doubt the women would already have fires going. Likely somebody would ask them to sit down a spell and have hot coffee. Strange to think that every day from now on, she would be seeing about as many people as ever got into the small church back home at Easter time. There'd be other folks to talk to. There might even be other babies, like Ann.

Isaac, going at a gentle trot, suddenly jerked back the reins so sharply that his horse reared, then whirled around.

"What's wrong?" Nancy cried. "Is it—Injuns?"

"It's Sapling Grove." He pointed. "I can see it written on that board over there. Nancy—this is *it*."

As the wagons came rolling up, as each of them saw and understood, they were stunned and silent. They stood at the edge of the clearing and stared between the trees at the five straggly horses, two wagons, a barrow, and one lone tent. They saw half a dozen men idling there, and one sorry-looking mule, waiting to go west.

5

★★★

"Where is everybody, Sam?" Sadie's voice had a sour twang. "You said at least fifty wagons! You said a few hundred people were going. Where are they all, Sam?"

Sam frowned and said, "Now, Sadie."

Lindy Gray smiled her vacant smile and murmured, "Maybe we're early?"

Nancy had dismounted, and she held Ann balanced on her hip. The baby, sensing her alarm, began to whimper and fret.

Ben whirled around angrily. "Nancy, can't you hush that child?"

She saw the tiredness in his eyes and held back a harsh retort. It had been mainly Ben's idea to join a wagon train. Even if the others said nothing, Ben would feel they blamed him.

Ben, too, would be wondering what was to become of them now. Go back home to be laughed at? Go back home—to what? One thing was sure; they couldn't go west, not just these few broken-down wagons. They hadn't nearly enough riflemen to fight off Indians, and numbly Nancy remembered Ma's warning, "There is no road to California."

Beside her, Isaac let out a low chuckle. "Looks like here comes a member of the great Western Emigration Society!" His voice was warm again, and humorous.

"Hold on," Ben chided. He turned to Nancy. "That's John Bidwell, the schoolmaster I told you about."

A tall young man, no more than twenty, strode toward them, smiling as he approached. "Hullo! So glad to see you folks." He extended his hand. "Kelseys, isn't it?"

Nancy felt a quick twinge of pride as Ben and John Bidwell shook hands, and Ben spoke for everyone, ending, "We all expected a bigger group."

"So did we, friend." Bidwell nodded. "But we've got some fine fellows so far, and with you folks, I guess we've more than doubled our number. We'll be expecting more people in a few days. Why don't you bring your wagons round and meet the others. Oh," he said, as an old man came shuffling up, "this is my partner, George Hinshaw."

The old man was thin as a rail. He muttered, "How 'do," and was immediately seized with a fit of coughing.

"Mr. Hinshaw is going west for his health," John Bidwell explained.

"And you, Mr. Bidwell?" asked Sam.

"I'm just off to see the country," Bidwell said cheerfully, touching the brim of his cap to Sadie. "I've been roving about the east, teaching school now and then. If it suits me in California, I will settle there."

Nancy had not realized she was staring at John Bidwell, but he caught her at it and flashed her a brief smile. Nancy quickly averted her eyes, embarrassed at having noticed how tall he was, and how he carried himself, like a man about to give a speech. She'd known a schoolmaster once before. She'd gone to school herself, parts of two winters. She figured it was learning that made a person so sure of himself.

They brought their wagons around to the edge of the creek. Then John Bidwell fell to introducing everyone. Nancy felt dizzy from the heat. Her arm ached, and Ann was not only hungry but also sopping wet. But it wouldn't do to excuse herself now. She might shame Ben by seeming unmannerly. So as each man was introduced, Nancy copied Sadie and Lindy, giving a slight nod.

There was Talbot Green with the fancy shirt and the broadest smile imaginable. He took his hat clean off to the ladies and held it to his chest. You could tell by the glitter of his gold tooth that he was a city man.

Next came two trappers, full-bearded and tough, dressed in leather. One was Charles Hooper, with a queer but friendly twitch to his mouth. The other was Grove Cook, steely-eyed and thin-lipped, his expression deadpan.

There was another young schoolteacher, Nick Dawson. He had no whiskers yet, only a faint shadow at the sides of his face. A stray dog followed at his heels, and he tossed it a tidbit or two.

Josiah Belden reminded Nancy of one of the shopkeepers back home. He was brisk and friendly, and his eyes moved rapidly over all the Kelseys. He knew for a fact, he said, that a dozen more men were coming. One was a Colonel Chiles who'd been to Florida as a volunteer and knew a lot about trails. No doubt, he'd show them all the way to California.

"We don't need no colonel to tell us," cried out a huge, heavyset man. As he spoke, he raised both arms, thick as hams, calling for attention. "I'm John Bartleson," he said with a nod toward the Kelseys. "I've got a map to California. You've got nothing to worry about, ladies." Bartleson gave a sudden smile in Lindy Gray's direction, and from the corner of her eye Nancy could see her blushing.

Nancy whispered to Ben, "I've got to feed the baby. Did you hobble Lightning?"

"He's all right." Ben looked irritated.

As Nancy walked back toward the wagon, she looked longingly at the creek. But the baby had begun to cry now in earnest.

Inside the wagon under the canvas cover it was stifling hot. A large horsefly buzzed and beat its wings against the canvas. As Nancy unbuttoned her bodice, she realized her body was coated with dust. Ann began eagerly to drink, and Nancy leaned back against the side of the wagon.

From outside she could hear the men talking, and then Lindy's high-pitched laughter. Yes, they would already be sweet-talking her, having discovered that she was a widow.

Once Nancy had asked Ben, "Do you think Lindy's pretty?"

He had replied as her mother would, tartly, "Pretty is as pretty does."

Nancy had persisted. "But isn't her face pretty?"

"Yes," Ben had admitted. Then he had grinned at Nancy. "I like my women larger, and strong."

Strong, Nancy thought. Was that why Ben had married her? Because she was strong? Probably she'd never know.

Again Nancy heard Lindy Gray's laughter, and she could picture Lindy's small nose and soft brown eyes. Lindy's hair shone the color of copper; it curled gently around her face. Men took a fancy to curly hair and soft eyes, Nancy thought. Her own eyes were sharp as a hawk's, and gray-blue. Nancy's hair lay thick and straight as that of an Injun squaw. It would never curl. Resentfully she pushed aside a stray lock.

Ann fussed and kicked. What had gotten into her? She was usually such a good baby. The heat, Nancy thought, lifting the canvas a bit. Sweat coated her body. She swallowed again and again, thinking of the cool water from the creek. Suddenly the baby gave a retch and spit up a thick stream of curdled milk all over the two of them.

Day after day they waited. Each day only one or two travelers came riding slowly into camp. Everyone would question the newcomers. "You got friends coming? Did you see other folks on the road?"

"No. No. Just us'n." They'd look around, resentful or angry. "Where's the Western Emigration Society?"

"This is it, friend. We're it."

Then suddenly in a single day nearly thirty people came. Wagons, horses, mules, oxen—they came into camp with a great noise and cheering, and for the first time it seemed really possible that they would make a trail west. By the end of the week over sixty people had gathered. To Nancy's joy, two of them were women.

Mr. and Mrs. Williams didn't say why they were going west. They kept modestly to themselves, and their sixteen-year-old daughter, Jessica, did not speak at all for the first two days. Then Nancy came upon her at the stream, washing clothes.

"Howdy."

No answer, as Jessica continued wringing out a pair of britches.

"Hope this is the last bundle of wash before we move out," Nancy said. Still, the girl remained silent, and Nancy wondered whether she ought to leave. She had so hoped they might be friends. Now she only stared back, wondering what to say next. Nancy had had a friend once before, but that was long ago when she was nine and going to the village school. Then, she'd known exactly what to say, and the two of them had chattered and laughed until the schoolmaster threatened to whip them.

"If I'm bothering you," Nancy continued uncertainly, "I could go on . . ."

"No!" It was a little cry. "I'd like to hold your baby. I'm all done wtih my wash. She's such a sweet little thing!"

"I'd be obliged," Nancy said. "I don't like to set her down, what with insects and all. . . ."

She glanced again at Jessica, handed her the baby, and waited, wondering what it was about Jessica that made her seem both so familiar and so strange. Her eyes were green and her hair was red as a fox pelt. It had been wrapped around her head to stay smooth, but small ends escaped and frizzed into tiny curls. Though she was dressed in drab gray homespun, Nancy got the feeling of bold, bright colors when she looked at Jessica.

"You don't look hardly older than me," Jessica said suddenly, "and you've got a baby."

"I'm seventeen," Nancy said.

"Well, I think it must be the nicest thing in the world to have a sweet little baby like this." Jessica broke into a grin. "Guess I'll never know about *that* 'cause my pa says likely I'll never get married. I talk too much. Pa says a decent, God-fearin' man wants a woman can keep her mouth shut. So I've tried, Nancy, I've tried my hardest not to say a *word* since we got to Sapling Grove, but I guess it's like to *kill* me staying quiet so long, and I'd rather be an old maid forever than go on trying. Ma says my tongue must be loose on both ends, and maybe she's right. She says nobody's going to stand being near me 'cause I do talk the sap right out of the trees. But, I'm thinking, if I *could* get married and have myself some babies, why then I'd have somebody to talk to who likely wouldn't mind at all 'cause they'd be just like me, wouldn't they? Except," she said with a sigh, "Pa says I won't ever shut up long enough for anyone to ask me."

For a moment Nancy only stared at her. Then she burst out laughing as she hadn't done in ages. Never had she heard such a tumble of words. Never had she seen such changing flashes of expression, except in a spunky kitten. Now, smiling to herself, Nancy realized what had struck her so familiar about Jessica—the eyes. Kitten's eyes, mischievous and solemn both at once.

"But, Jessica, it's possible," she said, "someone would *like* to hear you talk. Seems to me that just because your folks don't set a great store by talking, there's others that do."

Jessica gave out a little gasp of amazement, and her green eyes widened, like an owl's. "Why, Nancy Kelsey, I never thought of it that way. I really believe you might be . . ."

A commotion of angry voices made them both turn toward the wagons, where the men were grouped.

"They've started the election!" Nancy cried. She grabbed Ann. "Let's hurry!"

Jessica rushed to her feet, and as they went she muttered, "My pa says Mr. Bartleson acts like he's already been elected captain. Acts like he owns this whole wagon train."

"Well, he's got the most men in his mess. Eight rifles."

"That don't give him cause to lord it over people." Jessica flashed a grin. "He looks like an ox."

Nancy held her tongue. It near took her breath away to

hear Jessica talk like that. It made her smile a little, too.

"We need a captain," Colonel Chiles was saying as they approached, and Nancy settled herself beside Ben. "Someone with experience and good judgment."

"How 'bout yourself, Colonel?" Josiah Belden stepped forward, and his suggestion was echoed by Talbot Green and young George Shotwell.

"John Bidwell's got enough learnin'," someone called out. "He helped put this group together. Seems a good choice."

Ben nodded and spoke out, "I'm for Bidwell."

"Well, he don't know how to get there, does he?" Grove Cook's steely eyes narrowed, and he swung his arm truculently. "Book learnin' don't show us how to break a trail."

"Now, folks," said Josiah Belden, trying to keep peace, and in that moment a heavy arm was thrown around his shoulder and John Bartleson, sweating heavily, boomed out, "Now, boys, there's no sense wasting our breath about this. If you don't elect me captain I ain't going. And if I don't go, none of you can. I've got eight riflemen with me. I've got two extr-y oxen. I've got the map that shows how to get there, and my friend, Mr. Nye, has a letter from Dr. John Marsh who is already in California, telling how to go."

For a moment he stood silent; then he tapped himself on the chest. "I don't go following any man," he shouted, made confident by the silence. "This here is going to be the Bartleson Train, or you can all go sniveling back home."

Nancy stifled a gasp. Her face felt flushed as she stood beside Ben, feeling his rage, too, at this blackmail. For a moment she clenched her teeth, wishing Ben would shout out, "The devil with you, then!" to make them all know that the Kelseys couldn't be pushed around. She glanced at Ben and saw the muscle in his neck tighten and throb. Then, firmly he spoke.

"Mr. Bartleson, if you're going to be captain, we have a right to ask you about the route."

Bartleson tossed his head, laughing. "We just follow the

river! We just head due west, till our toes touch the Pacific!"
Behind him Grove Cook laughed, too, a low, rattling sound.

"That's not good enough for us," Ben said, his jaw firm.
"We've got to know the route." He turned to Michael Nye.
"How does this Dr. Marsh say we should cross the mountains?"

"Mountains?" Michael Nye looked puzzled. He spread out
the ragged letter, gazed at it, then said, "We're supposed to
look for the river that cuts through the Sierras. We're supposed to make canoes and float down into California."

Old Mr. Hinshaw let out a long donkey laugh, collapsing
into a cough.

"The mountain men don't tell of any river," grumbled
Charlie Hooper. "I heard Dr. Marsh never even came across
the plains. He got to California by sailing around the horn.
How would he know about any river?"

Nancy's heart began to pound as voices rose and men began
to shuffle their feet and clench their fists.

"You calling my friend a liar?"

"Maybe."

"You calling Mr. Bartleson here a liar?"

Deep within Nancy's body there began a fluttering, sink-
ing, terrible feeling. She wanted to close her eyes, clap her
hands over her ears, and scream out, "No! I won't go anywhere with you all!" She wanted to cling to Ben, beg him to
take her home, away from these crazy strangers who had no
real plan at all, just a wild notion to follow the sun.

Barely moving her lips, whispering so that only Ben could
hear, Nancy spoke. "Don't let them do this, Ben."

Nancy could see Ben weighing it, deciding whether to speak
up or stay silent. But it was Andy who cried out, Andy who
had been standing off on a rise and saw the dust cloud and the
rider, his horse nearly skidding in haste, his hat waving fran-
tically so that everyone knew the huge importance of his
message even before he screamed it out. "Wait up! Wait up!
If you need a guide, they're comin'. They know the way.
Wait up!"

6

★★★

They were missionaries, said the rider, bound for the Flathead Indian country in Oregon. They had an experienced guide, Thomas Fitzpatrick.

Even as the newcomers approached with their cumbersome carts and pack mules, those at Sapling Grove hastily completed their election. Talbot Green, with his handsome smile, was made president, for Mr. Weber, a tradesman with a love for order, said every company needed one.

"What is the president's job?" asked Nick Dawson innocently.

"Well, he takes care of . . ." Weber fumbled with his pockets, "he rather administers . . ."

It didn't seem to matter. Everyone was pleased with Talbot Green. They elected John Bidwell secretary. He would keep a diary of the trip. Actually, he had already begun. Several times Nancy had seen him sitting on a rock or log, pencil poised. She admired the way he could concentrate.

"We'll have to make some rules," stated Joseph Chiles, standing very erect. "We'll need to assign guard duty and . . ."

The sharp braying of donkeys from afar caused a restless stirring. Derisively, John Bartleson spat. Even Ben looked a trifle disturbed at the thought of newcomers.

Andy, hotheaded as usual, called out, "We don't aim to wait for no fuddy-duddy preachers!"

"Aw, shut up, Andy," yelled Sam.

"I don't blame him," shouted Grove Cook.

"You git out of family business, you hear," warned Sam,

☆ **35** ☆

itching for a fight. Nancy could see Sadie's lower lip thrust out in disgust, and for once she couldn't blame Sadie.

Bartleson took up the argument. "They'll slow us down with their singin' and prayin'." He swayed in comic imitation. "Probably won't even ride on Sundays. I say we move . . ."

But Charles Hooper came forward, his great shoulders seeming to cast a shadow over the entire group. "I've heard about Thomas Fitzpatrick," he said strongly. "Broken Hand, they call him. He's a good guide, known in the mountains as one of the best. I say we wait up, if the missionaries will have us. I say we're damn lucky." He glanced at the Kelseys and answered Ben's firm nod. "The Kelseys agree," he stated, ignoring Andy's look of outrage. "It's crazy to go without a guide."

Hastily Talbot Green mounted an old barrel, and he called, "We'll vote. Let's hear it! All for teaming up with the missionaries . . ."

There came a flood of "Ayes," and a fluster of "Noes," fading quickly as they were defeated. Green flashed his golden tooth and declared, "We wait for the guide!"

They waited in a self-conscious circle, aware of the disorderliness of their wagons, the twitching of their animals, the grime of their clothes.

As the missionaries came into view, Nancy felt a pang of embarrassment. She had not been to a church in over a year.

Even Bartleson stood silent before the spectacle of the approaching priests. There was something astonishing in the slow, steady plodding of their feet, the upward tilt of their chins, the swaying of the heavy crosses that fell into the folds of their long black robes.

Even Grove Cook's usually tight-set lips parted in surprise when Father De Smet lifted his hand and called, "Peace betide you!" and he beamed at them, splendid with his shock of graying hair and eyes that shone silver-blue.

Behind him came two other priests and eleven assistants, all silent, faces set in determination to save the redskins from eternal hell.

Talbot Green told of their wish to travel together.

Father De Smet moved close to the guide, Fitzpatrick. He stood whispering into his ear. They made a curious contrast, the dark-robed priest with his face miraculously smooth and pink, beside the grizzled mountaineer, bearded and wilderness-hard, dressed in leather and raccoon.

Fitzpatrick looked nobody in the eye. He glanced sidelong and tense, on the lookout for snakes or coyotes, or he squinted to the hills, expecting Indians or bear. His maimed right hand hung at his side. His left held a rifle that looked as if it had seen hail and fire aplenty, but still shot straight, smooth, and true.

Fitzpatrick listened to the priest. He mumbled. He nodded. Then he said, "Yup. They kin come."

Still they waited for everyone to get provisioned. The missionaries mended their carts and washed their clothes. Nancy, Jessica, and Lindy boiled down wild chokecherries and crab apples, making jelly. There was more company and more talk than Nancy had had in her entire life. Even Lindy opened up some. Away from the men, she left off her airs. Lindy, too, loved to listen to Jessica.

Ben was busy all day making extra ox shoes, tarring wagons and such. By evening he brooded, and when Nancy came to tell him some of Jessica's tales, he snapped crossly, "Seems you got nothing to do but gossip."

She drew back, breathing heavily. "Seems you got nothing to do but find fault," she said.

He mellowed. "I'm sorry, Nancy. I'm glad you've got a friend, and Jessica is right pert. It's just that we keep stalling. Those missionaries are going on a trail to Oregon. But we've got to go further where there is no trail. They might not be in any hurry, but winter can catch us, and then . . ."

"Winter!" Nancy stared at him, amazed. "Ben, you're talking silly. It's still middle May."

He squatted down by their fire and motioned her toward him. "It takes three months, maybe four," he said, "to cross the prairie and then the great desert. Nobody really knows how long. If we make a mistake and get on into October . . ."

A heaviness settled inside Nancy. She felt ashamed for her foolishness, giggling with Jessica, preparing sweets. She'd had no mind for serious things, for sharing the worries.

"Ben," she whispered, "listen, they say we'll pass buffalo. I heard Bidwell talking to that Englishman, Romain. We'll take lots of buffalo skins. We'll dry the meat and keep warm with the fur, so even if it gets to be winter, we'll be safe, won't we, Ben?"

Concealed by darkness, for he had kicked out the last of their fire, he nodded slowly and put his arms around her. "Yes, yes," he said, leaning his head down. "Now, when we start out, I want you to ride behind our wagon, to mind our things. It's going to be hard on you," he mused, then shrugged. "But you're strong," he added briskly. "Strong as an ox, I guess!"

Strong as an ox, as an ox, an ox. It was right good to be strong, wasn't it? As an ox? An ox? Nancy thought of it as she rode, holding Ann in her left arm, dutifully watching the end of their wagon, ready to holler for Ben should the ropes loosen and things tumble out, or an axle or a wheel break.

She had imagined it would be different; they'd ride along slow and easy, talking together, laughing. But no. It was work to keep moving. Even the kids had their chores. Little Mary was given a bag for picking up sticks and twigs along the way. Sam's boys took turns guiding the oxen, and the younger two had to work at sitting quiet in the cart with Sadie, being good.

That was the first two weeks, the easy time when there was still a clear road, rutted and muddy though it was. Their carts stuck fast in it, and it took half a day with everybody shouting and the horses straining to get them unstuck. Still, the guides and the priests said this was the easy time.

"Plenty of water and firewood," beamed Father De Smet, unperturbed that an entire cart with its contents—books, dishes, linen—lay broken and mired in mud. "It will mend, if the Lord wills," he said, and one had to believe him. He had, it was said, made this same journey twice before.

At the end of each day Fitzpatrick called out their miles, though how he knew, nobody could say. "Twenty-one miles —oh, a good day's trek! Now pull in."

They would drive their wagons into a great circle and picket the animals inside. Then came the rush to start fires, to bring pails of water from the river, and for Nancy there was always an extra job—the baby.

By night, in those first weeks, tales were told around the fires. Nancy listened and listened, her eyes wide, heart pounding. George Shotwell, slow and rambling, told how his ma scraped together a living raising chickens, how he needed to get out, how he told her good-bye and she just leaned on her hoe and said, "Mind you change your boots now and then, boy," for she'd left off opposing him when she saw the need in his eyes.

Smoking, sighing, not asking for sympathy, Joseph Chiles spoke of his wife who had died. "So I joined up . . . Florida campaign . . . married barely seven years . . . four young'uns." Friends took them in. What could he do? Now his son was a fine lad of sixteen, and the girls were turning pretty. "All these years I've been wanderin'. Heard Bartleson was lookin' for riflemen; here I am."

There were other stories that made Nancy's breath catch in her throat, and then the gay tales of Bidwell, Dawson, and Belden, looking for a lark and game to try anything. A week out, and another man joined them. He was John James. Everyone called him Jimmy-John. Tall, skinny, with a wide grinning face well creased from laughter, Jimmy-John arrived with a whooping and a robustness that made everyone grin and get a new surge of energy. He brought a fishing pole, a small leather-bound notebook, and best of all, he brought a fiddle. After that, some nights there'd be fiddle songs, and it was fine to lie out under the stars and listen.

In the morning Fitzpatrick's call came like a thunderclap over the stillness. "Get up! Get up! Get up!"

Nancy struggled to awaken. The sky was still black, and the stars distant. It was freezing cold. With stiff fingers she fumbled for her shoes, then for matches.

"Ben!" Nancy caught his sleeve as he returned from the river, carrying a bucket and lantern. "Are the oxen safe?" It was her first question every morning. Twice they'd already broken loose and had to be hunted down.

Ben nodded. "Help me with the tent. We've got to hurry."

"Can't you wait, Ben?" The matches were damp. Six of them flared momentarily, then went out. Ann began to scream hungrily.

"Nancy! What's wrong with you? Haven't you even got that fire started?" Ben snatched up the matches, and on the first try he succeeded in lighting a handful of dry blueberry brambles. "Now, the tent," he said grimly.

"I've got to feed Ann."

"She can wait. Your precious Lightning broke his hobbles again. I'll have to go find him."

"Oh, Ben, we'll be last. . . ."

"Maybe not. Just forget about fixing coffee. Get me some johnnycakes later. I'll try to hurry."

Hurry, hurry, or they'd miss breakfast or be last in the train, and last in line ate dust all day. Last in line got left behind, with nobody to help with a river crossing.

"Ben!" she called in the darkness. "Will there be a river crossing today, do you think?" She tried to keep the terror out of her voice.

"I don't know," he said tensely. "I guess not, Nancy," he added. "Probably not."

Nancy hurriedly fed and changed the baby, then bundled up their bedding and put everything inside the wagon.

"Nearly daybreak!" rang out Fitzpatrick's voice.

Ben—where was Ben? Usually he'd mind Ann while she went down to the river. Bracing Ann against her hip, Nancy picked up the bundle of soggy, smelly rags. Lord, if she were finicky, she guessed she'd die of embarrassment out here on the trail, dragging wet and messy breechcloths all over creation.

"Ben!" She squinted past the circle of wagons. She sighed heavily. Not one of the Kelseys was around. Confound it! She quickened her steps nearly to a run, muttering under her breath, anger rising. A person couldn't even get two minutes alone . . . not a speck of privacy . . . and Ben running off . . .

"Mrs. Kelsey! Can I help?"

"Oh!" Nancy drew back, astonished and flustered. It was Nick Dawson, leading his white horse, Monte. "I could mind that baby for a minute," he said, glancing over his shoulder, then offering his arm. "I'm obliged to you," he reminded her, "for tending Monte's leg the other day."

Gratefully Nancy smiled and placed Ann in his arms. "Thank you."

Tactfully he turned away, leading his horse downstream behind a clump of trees.

Nancy swished the rags through the icy water, straining on tiptoe to keep her shoes dry as she bent over the edge of the river. "That'll have to do," she muttered, pausing a moment longer to wash her hands and dry them on her skirt.

For a moment she felt a pang of despair. She had spent hours making this skirt, laboring over the sash and pockets. Now it was spotted and stained. In California, would she ever find cloth for another?

Perhaps on Sunday, she thought longingly, they'd stop and rest, and she could sneak in a bit of wash. Maybe the priests would suggest stopping. If not, maybe that strange new Methodist preacher, Williams. Yes, he was always jawing against sin and wickedness. No doubt he'd rather be hog-tied than miss his Sabbath.

Ben was waiting for her beside their wagon, with the oxen

already yoked. His face was red and scowling after his chase. Lightning lowered his head, nuzzling Nancy's hand expectantly.

"Don't you go giving him any treats!" Ben said angrily. "Broke those hobbles—I had to chase him a mile or more."

"Did you whip him?" Nancy shouted back, furious. She knew he had, and she was about to rail at him. Then she remembered that Ben hadn't even had a bite to eat. Her anger melted as Fitzpatrick's cry came surging over the meadow.

"Wagons! Moo-oove out!"

The call merged into the other sounds of morning. Wheels creaked. Hooves clinked. The grumbling of drivers and grunting of animals all blended into one great forward straining, and again came the captain's call, "Moo-oove out!" For a time everyone was silent, struggling to settle into the pace. Later, it became a rhythm.

Nancy had managed to begin the ride beside Ben, engaging him in conversation to catch him unaware. She did not like to ride behind the wagon. Besides, nothing ever did slide out. Ben was just too fussy.

"Know that Reverend Williams?" she told him. "I heard he's sixty-three years old. I heard he's got sixteen kids back home. Been married twice. Man his age—I wonder what made him come out like that to go preachin' in the wilderness."

Ben, trudging along, kept a sharp eye on the road. They were about middle in the train, but still a rut or a rock could cause a breakdown.

"Guess having sixteen young'uns," Ben said, his lips twitching, "is enough to make even a saint leave home."

"He says he had a vision. Told him to come out . . ."

"Now, there's a vision for you." Ben grinning, nodded toward Nick Dawson, astride one of Bartleson's mules.

"Hey, Badger, not so fast!" screamed Dawson. His legs flapped as the mule sped forward. Suddenly the animal stopped dead, sending Dawson flying to the dust. If a mule could laugh, Nancy thought, this one was sure doing it. Pawing the ground, it gave a long, taunting bray.

"Thunder and tarnation!" cried Dawson, grabbing the rope reins. "What'd he do that for? Hold still, you confounded, contrary, yellow-livered son of a . . ." Noticing Nancy, the young schoolmaster straightened his hat and mumbled, "Beg pardon, ma'am." He gave Ben a sideways glance. "I guess this mule has taught many a man how to cuss."

"Mules like to do the opposite of what you want," remarked Ben. "I'd rather use oxen."

"Oh, I prefer horses," said Nick, walking beside them, leading the mule. "But I thought best to stay off Monte another day, let his leg heal. So I'm off hunting, with the Badger."

Again he mounted the mule. Quickly Nancy called, "Mr. Dawson!" but the mule had already thrown Dawson again. This time he was sprawled out and obviously bruised.

Nancy glanced at Ben. She could hardly keep from laughing herself, and Ben's lips were twitching furiously.

"Mr. Dawson!" she called again. "I think the Badger is trying to tell you something."

Nick Dawson looked astonished. "How's that?"

"I think if you were to sit farther back, Mr. Dawson, and pull up the saddlebag. He's getting hit in the belly every step he takes."

"Is that so!" Dawson exclaimed. Once again he mounted, pulling himself well back in the saddle and tucking up the bag. "Well, now," he said, smiling contentedly, "you sure do have a way with critters, Mrs. Kelsey. I do admire it."

"My wife's always had a way with animals," Ben said. "She broke this here ox to the yoke herself."

Nancy felt a powerful, warm glow of pleasure inside her; she gave Ann a tight hug. Suddenly Ben called out brusquely, "You'd best go ride behind the wagon, Nancy! We're coming to some high ground, and I don't want our stores falling out!"

This time, she didn't mind riding alone. While she rode, her mind wandered back to when she was a little girl tending her mother's chickens, then helping her pa with the lambing. Her pa had said, "You got good, strong hands, girl, and a way with animals. Not to get proud—the Lord gives everybody something."

Nancy looked down at her hands, planning how she would fix a good stew at nooning. Yes, fix a stew and maybe lie down a spell in the cool grass—maybe take time to dust poor Ann with some herb talcum, where her skin was getting red from heat and chafing. Yes, at noon . . .

But at noon, just as all was settled in and peaceful, came the cry, "Indians!"

Only one word, it spread like wildfire. "Indians! Take cover!"

Nancy seized Ann. She ran behind the wagon and huddled there, covering Ann with her body, grasping a large rock.

"Indians!" Once more the cry, with all its terror. Then, silence.

7

From behind her wagon Nancy saw dust rising like smoke. She heard the pounding hooves of Indian ponies mingled with the high-pitched, searing cries of their riders, and again Nick Dawson's agonized shout, "Injuns! My God, hundreds of 'em!"

They were not the harmless Kansa, tame Indians who sometimes peered at the wagon train from behind trees and who wore white men's cast-off rags. These surging, yelping creatures were nearly naked. And painted. They held spears painted blood-red, dagger-sharp.

Nancy rose on her knees slightly, keeping Ann beneath her body, hiding her with her heavy skirt. Her legs began to tremble, while her arms were locked tight around the baby. She knew stories. True tales of redskins taking a white baby to swing it by the heels, smash its head against a rock, laugh to see the brains fly out. Once, long ago, a traveling man had shown Nancy and her pa the little scalp of a baby with tufts of blond hair. It made her vomit, and now the sour taste began in her mouth. She tried to swallow it down, choking on the dust.

Ben—where was Ben? Nancy squinted against the painful white glare of the sun. Sweat streamed down her sides.

The sharp crack of a rifle made her turn. Andy lay behind the priests' cart, taking aim. Beside him Grove Cook knelt, his mouth working, waiting for the Indians to reach the crest of the hill before he would shoot.

Noiselessly Ben slid down beside Nancy, breathing heavily. "Why don't they shoot?" She could hardly get the words out.

"I'm afraid they might!"

"But why are they waiting?"

The Indians had surged into position, spread along the edge of the hill overlooking the encampment, pausing for that moment before the full attack, and Nancy could see the glistening folds of their flesh, the slashes of red, yellow, and black, the steaming ponies, the silent faces, and hatred rose up in her stronger than any taste or smell or thought, and she gave a pull at Ben's rifle, wanting to scream out, "Shoot!"—wanting to pick them off one by one. . . .

Suddenly Fitzpatrick appeared. "Hold your fire!" The outline of his body seemed larger than life against the sun's white glare. For an instant Nancy felt overpowered, suffocated in heat. "Damn you greenhorns!" shouted Broken Hand. "Put those guns down! These are Cheyenne!"

"Cheyenne?" Nancy breathed. "But . . ."

Fitzpatrick whirled around, arms swinging, and he strode toward the Indians. He stood before them, legs outspread, fists clenched at his sides.

The loud, guttural words rang out. Indian talk, without meaning to Nancy, yet she did understand. Something in Fitzpatrick's tone and posture reminded her of Pa bawling out the kids, or Sam dressing down his boys before he went and got the strap. Thus Fitzpatrick confronted the Indians, meaning business.

The Indians began to ease up. They sat back on their ponies, sullen, staring. One of them nodded vehemently.

Slowly Nancy sat up. "Ben, I declare, he's *scolding* . . ."

But Ben was looking past her with a queer smile, and even Andy was shaking his head chuckling. Following their gaze, Nancy gaped, then blushed. There was Nick Dawson, crouched low, shivering like a rabbit, stark naked.

By the time Dawson reappeared, clothed again, everyone

stood clustered around the guide. Nancy's knees still trembled. She looked around, suddenly needing to know where everyone was. The priests were dusting themselves off. Mrs. Williams was weeping, and Jessica comforting her. Isaac stood awkwardly by, holding out Jessica's shoes. She'd taken them off at the nooning and left them during the scare. Sadie was furiously applying a switch to Luke's bare legs, and Luke was howling as expected, but not much hurt. Nobody really hurt. Thank the Lord. The Reverend Williams fell down on his knees, but only two men joined him. The others all turned to Broken Hand.

"We were waiting for the order to shoot!" Bartleson called critically, approaching the guide. "Why didn't you . . . ?"

"Had one ready in my sights," muttered Grove Cook. "I thought . . ."

"You didn't think at all," said Fitzpatrick sharply. "None of you."

Bartleson retreated, and Nancy saw him raise a dark flask to his lips and take a long pull.

"Cheyenne Injuns don't attack wagons," Fitzpatrick shouted. "These are just young braves, funnin' you. Probably out looking for some Pawnee squaws."

Dawson, nearly hopping with rage, pointed toward the Indians, placidly astride their horses. "They attacked me! They made me strip and they stole everything, right down to my boots!"

"They sure did," called Jimmy-John, doubled over laughing. "Never did see a man more naked!"

"Oh, you can laugh," Dawson fumed. "I might have been killed. It's this danged mule, ran right *toward* the Indians. They grabbed it, too. I had to run back to camp."

"And you led the Indians right back behind you," Fitzpatrick said dryly. Sternly he added, "Don't hunt alone. Learn to tell different Injuns apart. Cheyenne mostly like to play pranks."

Jimmy-John, still laughing, slapped his thigh. "Hey, Daw-

son, 'Cheyenne' Dawson, did you say there was a hundred of
'em?"

Bidwell took up the taunt. "Heaps of Indians, right, 'Cheyenne'?"

"Pranks," repeated Dawson. He managed a faint smile.

"I'll try to get your goods back," said Fitzpatrick, clapping
Nick on the shoulder. "We'll have a pow-wow tonight."

Lindy, sidling up, smiling prettily, asked, "What ever's that,
Mr. Fitzpatrick?"

The guide grunted. He avoided speaking directly to Lindy,
but turned to Nick Dawson. "You'll have to be ready to trade
with 'em to get your things back."

"What?" cried Nick. "Trade to get my own things back?"

Fitzpatrick shrugged. "It's their way." He raised his hand.
"Nooning's nearly over! You all learned something this noon.
Don't get trigger-happy. We can't afford it." He gazed down
at Nick Dawson. Then his mouth moved into a slow, unexpected smile. "Look's like you got yourself some traveling
companions. Those Injuns will follow you all day. Least you
got something out of it."

"What?" Nick asked, perplexed.

The smile became a grin. "A new name, 'Cheyenne.' "

All afternoon Nancy pondered it as she rode. They were
peaceable Indians. Broken Hand had said so. What was it
made some Indians peaceable and some so powerful mean?
And why didn't any of them ever smile? Or laugh? Wolves
didn't smile either, or wildcats, or any animals. She kept her
distance from the Cheyenne, even when the others gathered
close for the pow-wow, Lindy Gray laughing along with the
men.

That pow-wow! Never had Nancy heard so much shouting
and catcalling and laughing, with redskins sitting cross-legged
and passing the pipe, eating supper once and then again, for
redskins always ate twice, then palavering round and round;
Nick's britches were returned to him in trade for an old cap,
his boots for a plug of tobacco, and all the men roared with

laughter, Jimmy-John whistling and singing out until Preacher Williams got red-faced and very angry, thinking it more seemly to pray than to barter, and Nick swelled with pride and happiness at being the center of it all. In the end he got nearly everything back. Then Fitzpatrick got tired.

"It's a long day tomorrow," Broken Hand said. "By luck, we'll reach South Fork tomorrow noon."

"South Fork?" Nancy tried to sound casual. "Doesn't that mean . . . ?"

"Yes, Nancy," Ben said quietly. "But we've crossed rivers before."

"But the South Platte . . ." She stopped and busied herself with Ann's blankets. Yes, they'd crossed before. Each time the animals screamed and gasped, the men shouted curses, and Nancy forgot her intentions not to be scared.

"No two rivers are alike," said Jessica the next day. "That's what my pa says, and he's been talking to John Gray, that old mountaineer. He's a personal guide for that Englishman, Mr. Romain. They say he came along just to shoot buffalo. Imagine, hiring your own personal guide! That Englishman must be rich. Some of the men even call him 'Lord Romain.' You think he's really a *lord?* Seems like Lindy Gray's stuck on him. Of course, it seems like she's stuck on lots of men. Oh, I'm sorry, Nancy, I didn't mean . . ." Jessica clapped her hand over her mouth. "I do keep forgetting you're kin."

Nancy laughed. "It's all right, Jessica." Silently she rode for a time, with Jessica walking beside her. "Want to take a turn riding Lightning?" she asked.

Jessica shook her head. "No, thanks. My pa wouldn't . . . that is . . ."

"It's 'cause of my saddle, isn't it." Nancy nodded to herself. "Well, I surely won't ride sidesaddle all the way west. And, heavens, nobody can see even my stockings."

"Nancy, if they *could*," Jessica whispered, "I mean, if a man did see a girl's legs, would he . . . do you think he'd," she stammered, "take *liberties*, like Ma says?"

"I guess it depends on the man." Nancy fought the urge to tease. She'd seen Jessica peering at Isaac, waiting until he ambled toward the river before she herself would get water. More than once Mrs. Williams had been heard to exclaim, "Jessica! When in the world *will* you go for that water? I declare, I don't know what ails you!"

"Nancy, I wish I . . ." Then Jessica fell silent, and her cheeks blazed a deep red color.

Nancy pretended to concentrate on the road. She sighed slightly, remembering her own doubting and wondering. She remembered the feelings she'd had when she saw Ben from afar, maybe standing there just tethering his horse or come talking to her ma about some farm work, the feelings when her ma would say, "That Ben Kelsey's here again!"

"Well, I'm not scared of any river crossing!" Jessica tossed her head. "You going to unload your wagon?"

"We don't need to," Nancy said. "Ben built a false bottom, so all we do is hoist it up and tie it. Keeps our stores pretty dry."

"Unless the river's too wild," Jessica remarked, "I'm going to ride our mare across."

Nancy nodded. Ben had said he'd ride Lightning, and she could take Ann in the wagon. "You'll float, just as if you were in a boat," he'd said.

She told herself it would be easy. But after the nooning, the clouds began to turn from wispy white to smoky gray, like an omen. A chill wind began to push at their backs. It made the mules bray and the horses flare their nostrils apprehensively.

Nancy could not quell her uneasy feeling as she glanced up into the sky. *Was* it an omen?

"Ben!" she called, but he had reached the river's edge and could not hear her over the braying, stamping, and shouting that had already begun.

All was in a turmoil. Fretfully Lindy Gray stood holding Mary's hand, waiting for someone to help her across. Sam, poor Sam would make the crossing three or four times, taking all his kids. The men with mules retied their packs; others piled possessions into carts and covered them with rubber sheets, knowing they'd get wet just the same.

Jimmy-John, game to try anything, went first, and Nancy heard Bidwell call, "There's a brave chap! Best I ever knew."

For an instant even Jimmy-John hesitated. Fitzpatrick stood with one foot on the bank, the other braced on a rocky outcropping, and gave a forceful wave. "Get on! Hurry!"

Jimmy-John let out a blood-curdling yell. His horse whirled half around, then tossed its head high. Spurs struck. Screaming, the horse began its charge, white teeth and whites of eyes showing. Jimmy-John, gripping so tight that every muscle pulled taut, sank suddenly down to the horn of his saddle, and still Fitzpatrick cried, "Get on! Get on!"

Forward came Charles Hooper, Josiah Belden, George Shotwell, hats in their hands, then struck serious by the power of the river. It foamed and swirled, tearing out rocks as it went, pulling debris from the banks, tree limbs, then a boot, a pot, half a chair, as packs burst open and goods were claimed by the river.

"Mrs. Kelsey!"

Nancy felt numb, holding Ann, staring as one after the other of the animals were pulled into the water, cringing when they discovered the truth.

"There's quicksand," she breathed, then felt Ben's hand on her arm, and someone else was saying, "Hurry, Mrs. Kelsey," and helping her up into the wagon. Someone's hand boosted her up onto the platform, which rose high above the wagon floor, so high that her head nearly touched the canvas cover, and she sat crouched over holding Ann.

"Ben! Wait!" Her voice was lost amid the shouting, "Get on! Get on!"

Nancy felt one mighty lurch as Bright stepped into the water, and another as Buck moved forward. She could hear the shouts of Ben and Sam and Fitzpatrick, and the crackle of the ox whip. It never touched the beasts, but snapped over their heads, so terrifying that even the thundering river seemed better, and they strained forward.

"Get on! Get on!"

Nancy clutched the side of the wagon with one hand and a flour keg with the other, having thrust Ann down between her knees. The baby, strangely, lay very quiet, wide awake, her blue eyes staring. The wagon gave another mighty lurch, then creaked and groaned, as if the boards would crack apart. The swaying and the rocking, cracking and groaning went on and on, and from outside now Nancy could hear Lightning whinnying in terror and Ben—Ben who seldom blasphemed —cursing the horse, the oxen, the river, and all the dark days of his life.

Suddenly there came a great sucking sound. Ann's face went dead white, and in the next instant she began to wail. The wagon tilted and dipped, as if a great hand had slapped it sideways, causing the darkness to fall over Nancy, sending a roar into her ears, blotting out everything else—all sight, sound, thought, and feeling, with only panic left. She began to scream.

"Quicksand! Quicksand!" Did somebody shout it? Or was it her own voice? Nancy could only scream as the beasts sank down, down into the soft river bottom and the icy water began to seep up over the platform, touching her legs, her skirt, reaching higher. Instinctively Nancy grabbed the baby and held her up, screaming still. One of the wooden bows snapped in two. The canvas cover buckled and leaned crazily to one side. Now the icy water rose up, up over Nancy's body, up to her armpits, and as the water held her prisoner, she fell silent. Without words, she began to pray.

8

Somehow it ended. And as her terror ebbed, Nancy began dimly to remember her pa's drawling voice, explaining once to some city fellow about quicksand. "It's a fearful thing, quicksand. I've knowed it to suck under a cow. But then, cattle do panic. It's the panic that kills 'em, not the quicksand itself. Now, a horse'll leap right out at an angle, but an ox or a cow will struggle and make himself sink even faster. Gotta keep a cool head when you're crossing a river, yessir."

Ashamed, Nancy wiped her face with her hands. Beneath the frantic shouts of those outside the wagon, she felt a heavy inner silence. She had given way to panic, just like the dumb cows. Had she thought for a moment, she would have known that the men had tied ropes to the beasts to pull them out. She would have known that Ben would not let her sink. But she had not thought at all. She had screamed like a terrified lamb, like a child.

She straightened her shawl over her shoulders, forcing herself to breathe deeply. Her arms felt knotted and tight. She pulled the screaming baby down onto her lap, rocking gently, gently, to make herself composed and quiet. Thus, she waited for the men to bring her out.

George Shotwell's hand reached out to help her down, with Ben still seeing to the animals and Jimmy-John calling gleefully, "Right well done, Mrs. Kelsey! Wasn't that a fair adventure? Like to have another go at it, Mrs. Kelsey?"

She looked down at him from her height on the platform,

and she smiled brightly, as she'd so often seen Lindy do. "Why, I think not, Mr. John. At least, not this moment. It's only right to give someone else a chance."

Her heart pounded with relief and amazement at her own boldness. Ben would be proud, seeing she'd overcome her terror, and even Jimmy-John said she'd done well.

On firm ground again, Nancy felt a surge of joy and relief. "Ben!" she called.

"Dang it, the flour got wet!" he grumbled as the platform came down and he examined the stores. "And it looks like rain tonight. You'd better bake some biscuits right quick."

Yes, biscuits! Yes, Ben Kelsey, think of biscuits for your fat stomach, when I just about drowned and died! Angrily she turned, vowing to spice those biscuits nicely with a handful of cayenne pepper. But suddenly everything changed.

The general shouting took on a different tone. The uproar faded into a stunned silence, dragging out for a long moment before the noise rose again, this time in shouts of disaster.

Nancy saw the backside of the mare. She saw the flash of red hair, the glimpse of a foot caught high over the side saddle. For a moment she did not quite understand. Then understanding overwhelmed her.

The mare was so terrified that she was swimming downstream. The current caught and lifted the huge body as if it were merely the limb of a tree, hurling the horse straight toward the bristling boulders that, just beyond, divided the flow in two. Jessica, her foot tangled in the stirrup, hung like a dead weight, head down, bumping against the mare's surging flank.

"That horse! Look at it!" called Brolaski, one of the riflemen. "Musta broke its leg." He snatched up his rifle, turning quickly to the guide. Questions flashed between them. Shoot the horse and keep it from dragging the girl further? What if he missed and shot Jessica instead? Or if Jessica went down with the horse and drowned?

"Shoot over its head!" yelled Fitzpatrick.

The shot rang out—a diversion. In that same instant Isaac plunged his horse into the river in the path of the struggling mare.

Another shot echoed. Nothing seemed to change; still the mare flailed and was pulled downstream toward the jagged boulders just beyond Isaac; still Jessica's body hung down, flapping hideously against the horse.

In a single lunge Isaac, nearly out of his saddle, threw himself at the approaching mare. The impact sent him and his mount reeling sideways, but he had managed to turn the mare's head.

Suddenly, only the river was moving. All else was still. Somehow they got the horse out of the water and Jessica free. They laid her out, unconscious, on the muddy bank.

Nancy could only gasp, her eyes wide, staring. She gazed up, and now the prairie looming ahead was cruel and harsh and endless. It seemed beyond enduring.

Mrs. Williams sank down beside her daughter, rocking back and forth on her heels, hands shielding her face. "Oh, no. No, no, no, no. Not this last one, Lord. No, not my Jessica!"

She did not weep. The dry moans were more pathetic than tears, and her husband stood by nodding helplessly, patting her shoulder, saying, "Now, Mama. Now, Mama."

Nancy got a strange, lightheaded feeling. Jessica lay so very still, her face a pasty gray, her lips lacking all color. Even her hair, always bright as a flame, lay limp and mud-colored, the wet strands mingling with a thin ribbon of blood that flowed outward from the cut on her head.

Suddenly the Reverend Williams appeared, cloak flapping and hair standing out like a prickly bush. "Woman!" he called almost sternly, raising Mrs. Williams to her feet. Still she moaned and hid her face. The preacher bent over her. "This child of yours," he cried, "is the Lord's. Praise Him, even now, when he tries you sorely. The Lord loves your daughter even more than you yourself."

The woman turned to face him, her mouth twisted and

eyes wild with a great bitterness. "As He also loved the others?" she cried. "Are *your* children dead?"

"Mama, come, Mama," murmured Mr. Williams, leading her away. "Come, we've got to put her in the wagon." He cast a backward, apologetic glance at the preacher, who stood wiping his brow, his eyes feverishly red.

Ben, John Bidwell, and Captain Fitzpatrick made a litter from a blanket to carry Jessica. Watching, Nancy thought numbly, *My friend, my friend.* They would wrap her in blankets and cause her to sweat; perhaps that would break the stupor. They would let a cup of blood from her arm to draw out the poisons from her wound. And then . . . what?

Brolaski had been right. One of the mare's legs was broken. The other streamed blood from a huge gash, leaving a trail as the horse limped behind a copse of cottonwood trees.

Mr. Williams had gazed at the horse, then at Brolaski, who stood by with his rifle. Wordlessly Mr. Williams had nodded. Wordlessly Brolaski followed the mare behind the cottonwoods. They were low and sparse, so that when the shot rang out, nothing was concealed from the sight of the others.

Nancy's hands were trembling and her legs felt numb as she moved slowly, mechanically, to the privacy of bushes and boulders where she could tend Ann and nurse her.

The entire camp was subdued; even the sounds of the animals, in their exhaustion, were muted. Thus Fitzpatrick's cry rang out all the sharper, echoing like a shot, "Get ready, ready to moo-oove out!"

In disbelief, Nancy sprang up. People began to lead in their animals, to tighten girths, moving into position.

Aghast, Nancy sought Ben and found him at the river's edge, retrieving a broken box of nails.

"Fitzpatrick says to move," she sputtered, "but how can we . . ."

"Be there in a minute," Ben said, poking through the mud.

"But Jessica's hurt!" she cried. "We have to wait!"

"They can move Jessica in the wagon," Ben said, "or the

Williamses can stay behind till she gets stronger. It's up to them."

"But, Ben," Nancy cried, "why can't we all wait? What difference could a few hours make? She'll likely be better in a day or so. . . ."

"It's not my decision," Ben said, his jaw set. "All I know is that if we all stay back every time something happens to one of us, we'll never get there. The captain knows we've got to keep moving."

Father De Smet, having come to fill his water jug, nodded serenely. "It's true," he said. "A wagon train cannot wait. Our captain knows this as well as anyone. Once he even had to abandon his own friend." The priest nodded. "It was long ago."

Nancy fought to keep from arguing, but dark, angry thoughts persisted. A few hours' time in exchange for Jessica's welfare—maybe even her life? It was downright mean. She pressed her lips together, mounted Lightning, and took the baby from Ben. At least Ann was asleep. Nancy didn't think she could have tolerated a fussy baby now.

They moved out side by side, Lightning's pace matching that of Ben and the oxen.

"We'll soon hit buffalo country," Ben said.

Nancy knew he was only trying to make conversation, to pretend everything was pleasant. She refused to answer.

"They say there's hardly any wood out where the buffalo run," he continued. "But you can burn buffalo chips. Wonder, do they smell?"

Still Nancy remained tight-lipped.

"They say buffalo tongue's the best meat in the world," Ben persisted.

"They can't stay all alone!" Nancy suddenly cried out, all her anger exploding. "They need help to stand guard, and Mrs. Williams is so fretful. . . ."

"Well, they won't be all alone," Ben said with a strange smile. "Isaac's staying behind to help them."

"Then so could we!" Nancy cried. "Please, Ben!"

"No. I won't separate from this wagon train. Not with you and the baby. I'd never take that chance."

"You wouldn't!" She felt her body stiffen, her eyes blazing sharp. "What about me? Jessica's my friend!"

"And you're *my wife!*"

Truly vexed, Nancy bit her lip, thinking thunderous thoughts to accompany the ever darkening sky. *He* wouldn't take that chance. Never mind asking her how she felt about it. Never mind giving her any right to speak, her only friend likely to die . . .

"Tell you what, Nancy." Ben turned aside from the oxen. "After we make camp tonight, you bake some biscuits and fix something good for Jessica. You know, some of your herb tea. I'll ride on back to the Williamses and give it to her."

For an instant Nancy could only stare at him. Then feelings, stronger than either tears or laughter, flooded over her. "Oh, Ben!" she whispered, wanting to dismount, to go to him.

But he had already turned away, calling loudly to the oxen, "Ho, Buck! Ho, Bright! Make tracks!"

Just at dusk it began to thunder, and the few sticks of firewood soon gave out, leaving them in darkness and driving rain. Fortunately, Nancy had baked her biscuits quickly, setting the Dutch oven into the deepest, hottest coals. Then she prepared a strong lobelia tea, and Ben, despite the alarming weather, was true to his word.

He returned many hours after the others were silent in their tents, panting and soaked to the skin. He came into the tent, his hair dripping, but his face shining happy by the light of his lantern.

"Ben!" Nancy propped herself up on one elbow, instantly awake. "How is she?"

"Well, she's mending." He smiled, and she knew he'd draw it out, just to tease. He took off his water-logged jacket. "Right pert now, I'd say." He pulled off his boots. "She's talking."

"Talking!" Nancy cried gleefully. "Really, Ben? What'd she say?"

"Ain't anybody in the world can keep track of all Jessica Williams can say even in ten minutes!" He grinned. "But she's better, Nancy. They'll set out tomorrow. Might be caught up with us by tomorrow night. Mrs. Williams said to thank you kindly for the tea. She sipped a bit herself. Said it steadied her."

"Did Isaac say anything?" she asked.

"What do you mean, 'anything'?" Ben pursed his lips.

"You know perfectly well, Ben Kelsey. Did he say anything about Jessica?"

"Now, what in the world would he say? Said he'd stand guard for the Williamses tonight. That's what he said."

"Well." Nancy smiled to herself. "Well."

"What do you mean, 'Well, well'? I do swear, it's powerful hard to talk to a woman."

"Just be still then," she whispered, still smiling to herself as Ben put out the lantern and crawled in beside her under the pile of blankets topped by Ma's farewell quilt.

Things changed. Nancy's weariness at the end of a day's ride was different than before. It was more an old sort of weariness, overall aches like old people complain about, a film over the eyes, a squirming and itching uncomfortableness. It came from being out on the open prairie.

Even the young'uns changed. Their faces got a pinched, almost scared look. Before, while they were traveling alongside the rivers, with trees and hillocks all around, the kids would run and jump and catch some excitement from the dreary day. Now they stayed close, their eyes large and round, frightened not so much of Plains Indians as of the plain itself.

It was big. Big as the night sky, but without any breaking points like moon or stars. It was sameness-big, endless-big, giving off a smell and feel of its own. Dry, half-yielding grass underfoot smelled like earth cut and laid open by the plow, felt like baked clay or half-ripened hay stalks, slippery smooth, fresh, endless.

Endless, too, the waving, waving of the wild wheat, the steady blowing of a wind that seemed to come from nowhere in particular, but flowed on and on and on, changing only as it grew louder at times, a roar in the ears instead of a soft moan, but then one couldn't even be sure it had changed. Maybe it was only the imagination and the vast emptiness.

The wind was like a separate thing, neither living nor unliving, but a thing in between, like a ghost, invisible and restless. Blowing warm or hot or icy cold, it was always there. It bore midday heat as thick as the inside of an oven. It brought midnight cold as icy as the wildest blizzards. It made them weary. It made them irritable.

Nancy had not reckoned on the emptiness of the prairie. It was a sorrier thing than she had imagined. Even the song of Jimmy-John's fiddle seemed lost and lonely as it mingled with the prairie wind at night. Children's shouts were cast about, then swallowed up by that same wind. An entire wagon train could disappear, Nancy supposed, people and beasts and wagons together, and never be missed.

Sadie and Sam and Andy began to come round at night, sitting with Nancy and Ben. Like as not, the brothers would end up in a quarrel, but it didn't matter; they were kin. Groups formed. Four or five men, mostly come out alone, found friends to ease the bigness and the rawness of the prairie.

Ann changed. She began to sit with her eyes open wide, trying to reach, reach for something that wasn't there. Her little fists would clench, then straighten as she waved her hands as if reaching out to the waving grass. It was as if she, too, needed to grab onto something solid where there was nothing. Not a building, tent, stump of a tree. No trail, no broken-down abandoned wagons—nothing. Nothing marred the endless space except for the crisscrossing of crows overhead, or the sudden swoop of a gray hawk, and one day, a skeleton.

"Ben!"

"Sam!"

"Hey, Chandler!"

Friend called friend. They gathered to see. They knew it was not a human skeleton, but oh, what size of beast, with bones thick and bulging, the shoulder-blade bone as large as a shovel, the skull three times over the size of a bear's head.

"Buffalo." Father De Smet gazed at the bones. He picked one up, then laid it precisely back. "Soon we'll see the herd. The ladies," he said with a nod, "will find the robes useful, and also the chips. As to the meat . . ." He smacked his lips.

Soon they began to see the large round droppings of the buffalo. Leading Lightning, Nancy walked and began to pick up the "chips." They were dry and light and porous. They looked like flat, crusty mud pies. They would probably burn like pine cones, Nancy thought, gazing ahead.

Then she saw them. A mass of brown, as if the prairie had been scorched by fire. As she stared, the mass began to move slowly, the way a stain spreads out on cloth.

Now the others saw. Buffalo. They said it over and over. Buffalo. Whatever anybody had said, the first sight of buffalo told it different and told it all, so you'd never forget. They were simply *buffalo*, unlike any critters on earth, dominating the entire plain as if it had been made just for them.

Their hoofprints tore out huge chunks of sod, leaving deep holes and scars. The dark mass of beasts seemed to seethe and buzz with swarms of insects hovering around them, but they stood quietly, lazily switching, heavy manes bobbing up and down as if to say it was all too much, the flies too many, the day too hot under that matted, shaggy hide, so just abide.

And the smell! You could smell buffalo half a mile away. It was a sharp smell, unlike cow or horse or dog, but just *buffalo,* a smell you'd never forget.

For a long while the travelers only stood looking down at the grazing herd. Then Jimmy-John rode ahead, a gleeful yelp sending him along, rifle swinging from his shoulder. Brolaski and Chandler followed, scarcely able to keep up with Jimmy-John in his wild enthusiasm.

Fires were kindled in readiness for the kill. The hunters went out and were gone scarcely an hour when Jimmy-John rode into camp, subdued for once, speaking softly.

"We brought one down," he said. "Seemed like it would never fall. Took three shots in the heart, three more in the head. Beast kept moving. Walking toward me. Looking at me. Weird. Shot again two, three, four shots more. It kept comin'. Toward us." He paused, wiping sweat from his face. "That devil took twenty shots. Twenty shots until he fell."

In silence they all let it sink in. Twenty shots. The power of such a beast.

Ten of the men went to bring in the buffalo, to skin it and stretch out the hide as Fitzpatrick directed. Later they feasted on buffalo steaks and passed around bits of the prized tongue and brains, said to be delicacies. Nancy found the innards too soft and flavorless for her taste. But the steaks were delicious. She ate two large ones, thankful that they still had a bit of flour left for bread to go with it. Not long, though. Flour was already running out. Much of it had gotten wet during river crossings. Some molded. Some became infested with the same tiny brown bugs that bit them so maddeningly in the night.

"Good supper," Ben said, stretching out gratefully. "Delicious biscuits."

Nancy smiled contentedly. She had chewed up a bit of the meat and put the mash into Ann's mouth. The baby had swallowed a little. It would strengthen her, Nancy thought. Soon she must think of feeding her other than milk. Nancy decided to ask Sadie about it. But not now. It was too fine a night, and she felt too full and contented to move.

They bedded down happily, huddled together under the

blankets. The nights were freezing cold. Nancy smiled to herself; that didn't keep Isaac in! She knew he'd still be out in front of the Williamses' tent, pretending to be working out a swollen joint in his horse's leg. He'd gotten Jessica to help him. Her pa would poke his head out now and then to holler, "Gettin' right late, Jessica! Young man, you ought to let that horse of yours get a little sleep!"

Nancy whispered softly, "You think he's asked her yet?"

"Don't know what you're talking about," Ben replied.

"I'll bet you don't!"

Soon all was quiet except for the faint crackling of twigs from the men on watch, and then, from far off, a sound like thunder.

Like thunder it rolled, growing louder, until at once it seemed near crashing above them, but with no bright claps across the sky, no flaring zigzags of light, only the thundering, vibrating sound.

Lanterns began to blaze. Men rushed out with rifles slung over their shoulders. Old John Gray cried out hoarsely, "Stampede! Buffalo stampede!"

The word brought a flash of memory. Nancy had seen cattle stampeding once. The beasts surged like a living sea, trampling everything in their path, and afterward she had seen the broken bodies of young lambs and a shepherd dog mashed into the ground so that only hide and blood remained.

"Stampede!"

Like fragile sticks, their wagons would break under the huge hooves. The herd, gone wild, would follow its leader blindly, crashing over and through campfires, tents, wagons, people.

Now Nancy could feel the ground shaking beneath her. The roar rose about her like a cannon roll. Nothing could stand in the path of the galloping beasts.

There was no safe place to go. There was nothing to do but hang on to the trembling earth and wait.

9

In the morning, when it was over, Nancy knew it was one of the longest nights of her life. Longer even than the night she gave birth to Ann. The pounding of hooves and the booming of rifles was deafening. Men shot continually through the night to turn the beasts away from the camp.

Nancy had at last crept into the wagon. Peering through the slit under the canvas she could see flash after flash of gunpowder, mingling with the sparks that flew from the hooves of the buffalo, or so it seemed. Sight and sound blurred together; trembling, flashing, roaring, and shouting, all merged into a terrible, endless clamor.

She could not even hear her baby crying. She did not hear when Lindy approached, dragging Mary behind her. Lindy looked white as a ghost, her sleeves torn where branches had caught as she ran. Her arms and cheeks were scratched and bleeding.

"Lindy!" Nancy had led her down onto the quilt. She tucked little Mary in beside Ann, covering their heads to drown the awful noise.

"Lindy! What's wrong?" Lindy had never come to her before. Maybe the buffalo had already trampled the far side of the camp.

Lindy shook her head. "I've got nobody." The words came from the movement of her lips rather than from any clear sound.

She said nothing more. Her face was set as in stone, pale and grave. But all through the night Lindy's hand was tight on Nancy's arm, and while the guns roared and the ground trembled, Lindy only stared and shook her head.

At dawn the shooting stopped. People emerged from their wagons, disheveled, gray-faced. Talbot Green stumbled out, carrying some heavy load that he'd obviously clutched throughout the night. Old Hinshaw staggered and nearly fell. Everyone moved slowly, groggy from the noise and the night.

No tree or rock marked the place where the men had fought back the great beasts. Nancy looked down and saw only scarred earth, broken grass, and muddy footprints. A haze and a smell hung over the place, settling as after a great battle. Here and there empty flasks lay amid the broken prairie grass. They had surely been full to the brim with whiskey and swallowed down fast when the men were desperate and thought it their very last drink on earth. Back in Sapling Grove they had all made a pact. No whiskey would be brought out on the trail. The priest, gazing down at the ruin, murmured, "Ah, well." On such a night, his expression suggested, one could forget and be forgiven.

But Reverend Williams was furious. "No good account can come of evil ways!" he cried. "Drinking and swearing. Gambling and wickedness . . . if we held proper Sabbath . . . !" He shook his head angrily. His eyes were red, and he pointed out over the prairie, crying out, "See there!" implying that the travelers were somehow responsible for the wreckage left by the stampeding beasts.

They had cut a swath across the prairie, trampling and fouling the sod for miles. Horses, mules, and oxen nuzzled the ground. There was no grass left for them to eat. As for water, the river flowed sluggish from the filth left by the buffalo. The water was unfit to drink. Dead fish had already risen to the top, soon to add their stench of decay.

They moved out slowly, dejected, hungry. By noon their train was broken into three straggling segments, as much as two miles apart.

"It's the buffalo meat," said the trapper John Gray. Word spread along the line.

"My stomach's on fire," Ben told Nancy, half doubled over, though he continued to walk beside the oxen. "Gray says it does some folks this way. All Sam's boys are ailin', except for Luke. Poor Lindy's been down in her wagon all day, and Andy's driving it for her, bringing up the mules, too." He looked at Nancy quizzically. "You don't mind it?"

"The buffalo meat?" She smiled. "I loved it. And it seems to agree with me. I feel good."

Ben gave a sniff. "Strong stomach."

Soon afterward Ben gave up, running to the bushes. "Keep 'em moving!" he called back. "I'll catch up later."

By nighttime Ben was so sick with cramps that Nancy ran to get the captain. He was bedded down under a tree, rolled in a blanket. He looked up, his small eyes bright, and said, "It hits some folks like that. Tender stomachs. Make him retch."

Nancy gave Ben half a cupful of calomel. It did its work quickly. By morning Ben was pale and quiet, but the cramps had subsided. By the next day he was ready to eat again.

Most of them did begin to tolerate the new food, and some thrived on it. But Lindy Gray continued to suffer, despite calomel and lobelia and even a bit of quinine from the priest's medicine bag. Lindy's face was paler than ever, the skin nearly transparent at the temples. She seldom smiled, but held her lips tightly together, summoning all her strength to hide her misery from the others. But to Nancy she confessed one evening as they washed their things together at the stream, "Nancy, I feel like to die. I never had anything like this before. My insides are on fire."

"Did you take some of the broth I made you at nooning?" Nancy frowned, noticing again how frail Lindy looked.

"I tried, Nancy," she whispered. "Everything I eat makes me sick all over again."

"Let me take Mary for a few days," Nancy suggested. "I'll

walk Lightning and put Mary in the saddle. Billy and Jeremy are big enough to handle your team. It'll keep them out of mischief. You can lie in the wagon and get your strength back."

Lindy's eyes, wide and tearful, reminded Nancy of a doe. "Oh, Nancy, I couldn't. . . ."

"Nothing more about it," Nancy said briskly. "Mary will help me gather chips. It'll be nice to have somebody to talk to, walking along."

But the child barely spoke. She was a shy, wiry little girl, and tough, too. She never fussed, even when she fell headlong into a prickly pear with wicked, sharp thorns. She'd get along, Nancy thought, taking pride in the child, suddenly feeling close to Lindy as blood kin.

"Would you like to hold Ann?" she asked Mary, thinking to give her a treat.

"No, ma'am."

"Why not?" Nancy smiled down at her.

"Mary careless," the child said seriously. "Drop things."

Nancy nodded. "I don't blame you then. I guess it's too much for a four-year-old to be responsible." She laughed to herself and added, "At least you know enough not to bite off more than you can chew, don't you."

Solemnly the little girl nodded, and Nancy wished she could make Mary laugh or at least smile. The child's laughter came later that night, most unexpectedly, when Nancy would have imagined screams instead.

It had been a broiling hot day, so hot that Nancy had fallen asleep at nooning and awakened to find her bodice drenched with sweat. By afternoon, strangely, the sky had turned nearly black, with great clouds gathering and whirling like gigantic tumbleweeds across the sky, and the wind starting to blow so fiercely that wagons skidded and nearly turned over on their sides.

What happened next was so swift and extraordinary that Nancy could only gape, too astounded even to be scared. Ben had had the wit to picket their wagon down with stout ropes. They sat inside watching as the sky seemed to turn itself inside out. From behind them came a huge, whirling black waterspout, an enormous column reaching straight down from the sky, bringing with it such a storm as none of them had ever witnessed. Five wagons did turn over and lay splintered the next day. Half a dozen animals fled in terror and were lost forever. One of the men threw himself flat down as lightning began straight overhead, ripping across the black sky, brightening it like midday with a crashing that sounded as if trees were being torn out by the roots and split asunder.

Fast on the heels of the lightning came the thunder, then the deluge. Water poured down in torrents upon the flat land, forming surging pools and little rivers. Then came the hail. Hailstones clattered and rattled against wagons and rocks. Horses screamed out at the pelting hailstones and were heard even above the clatter.

Isaac, shouting, ran out into the storm, and Ben, too, had lost his sense, it seemed. He dashed out to meet his brother, and the two of them stood in the dark against flashes of lightning, being pelted by hail. They bent down to gather something, then ran their separate ways.

"Nancy!" Ben cried gleefully. "You've never seen the like! Look! It's the size of a turkey's egg!"

In his open hand lay the largest hailstone Nancy had ever seen. The sight of it sent Mary into peals of laughter. She began to suck at it, as if it were a piece of candy.

In the morning they saw how lucky they were. Their camp had been spared, although several trees had been struck by lightning. The ground itself yielded underfoot, water-logged as a sponge, sending up thousands of shiny black beetles.

The animals bucked and rolled their eyes nervously. Lightning pawed at the ground and ran from Nancy, tossing his head. At last she subdued him and saw the raw gash on the side of his neck, and a long red welt marring his glistening brown and white coat. Another horse had kicked him in its terror; a hoof mark stood out plainly on Lightning's rump.

"Poor thing," Nancy murmured, packing the sores with mud. "This will help. Now, now, hold still. It was a bad night." The horse nuzzled her hand and gave a long breath, like a sigh.

They set out slowly, for the long wet grass clogged spokes and axles, and mud weighted down the feet of the animals. Miraculously, by afternoon the sun had baked the earth dry. Crusts and cracks began to form. Nancy stared, amazed. It was, she thought, like watching a year of seasons happening in minutes before her eyes. She marveled at the blazing heat, and it did not bother her now. She began to wonder, really wonder, about the kind of power that could do such things.

She walked along, filled with her wonderings, so engrossed that she scarcely felt the weight of her baby or the pull of Lightning as she led him at a slow, thoughtful pace. Often she had noticed John Bidwell gazing up to the sky as he walked, his face heavy with pondering, or reading from a slim book of poems, stopping to think. Now she felt in tune with him.

It was all so strange. The world was so large. There was much to ponder. That dark column reaching down from the sky—was it the finger of God? Could a person see such a thing and live?

No, she decided. She gazed down at the tiny purple flowers that popped up unexpectedly among the wild grasses. No, she did not really think of God as a person—not since she was grown, anyhow. The preacher said He made all things. Then He made the storm, and plague, but He also sent the little purple flowers here, gave them a place to grow.

She frowned deeply, wishing she could think it all through, figure out how it was all connected. In the endless blur of days there was no time to think of such things. But now, a new idea seemed possible. It lay just beyond the edge of her thoughts, and she felt a surge of annoyance even at Jessica's interruption.

"Nancy!" Jessica ran to catch up. "I want to ask you a favor."

"Of course, Jessica." Reluctantly Nancy put aside her thoughts.

"I hope you won't think it's too forward," Jessica said, eyes downcast, "if I ask to borrow your bonnet. You know, the tan one. Just for one day. Really, just for an hour or so on Sunday."

"Well, Jessica . . ." Nancy's new bonnet lay in its store box wrapped in tissue paper. She had worn it only once on a Sunday to attend Reverend Williams's prayer meeting. Then she had carefully laid it away, planning to save it until they got to California. She turned to Jessica reluctantly. "I know you'd be very careful . . ."

The instant she met Jessica's eyes, so merry and fairly bursting with excitement, Nancy knew. She dropped the lead rope and, still holding Ann, threw her arm around Jessica in a joyful hug. "Jessica! What a way to tell me! When? When did he ask you? Oh, Jessica, and your folks are willin'? Oh, Jessica, we'll be *sisters!*"

Jessica scooped up the baby and held her tight, whirling around in her happiness. "We'll live right close, and our young'uns will play together. Ben and Isaac can farm together, and just think of all the times we can share! We'll never be lonely, and we'll help each other with barn raising and harvest, and we can quilt together, Nancy, and sometimes go to town. . . ."

All day Nancy was filled with the wonder and the beauty of it. Never again would bad news be quite so bad, or hard times so trying. Never again would loneliness come weighing upon her, like an animal presence, filling every space, making it hard to breathe. Things would be different. The Kelseys would be different, closer and kinder; Andy's temper wouldn't matter so much, or Sadie's bossiness, because Isaac and Jessica were so very happy. It would rub off on everybody.

It did rub off on everybody. It was a special day. For a

few hours on Jessica and Isaac's wedding day even the prairie seemed different. The blue sky made a wide canopy and the pale-green grass a carpet, and the wind blew gentle, like a song for the bride and groom. A small gray bird perched atop Ben's wagon sang out clear, looking down at the preacher in black and all the people standing so solemnly around the young couple.

Isaac's hair was slicked down, and his skin faintly tingled from a scrubbing. Jessica looked so womanly in her ma's gown of pearl gray with real lace at the throat and wrists, and her eyes shone blue with the blue lining of the bonnet, and her lips and cheeks were rosy with some special magic thing lent by Lindy Gray.

Nancy, Sadie, Lindy, and Mrs. Williams had put their stores together and baked a wedding cake. Without eggs or soda to lighten the dough, the cake made a heavy mass in the Dutch oven. But everyone said it was delicious, and Lord Romain shared a precious tin of sour balls, and Bartleson's men passed around something to keep themselves jolly.

Late through the night Jimmy-John's fiddle still sounded, and there was dancing, and even Preacher Williams didn't mind. Talbot Green, his teeth gleaming in the firelight, danced a Scottish jig, clapping his heels together in a high leap. Luke, beside himself with excitement at getting a new aunt, danced and hopped as nimble as a flea, until he fell asleep by the fire, exhausted.

By late night everyone was mellow with remembering other times and other weddings. Colonel Chiles began to murmur of his wife, so long dead. Charles Weber spoke of his grown daughters; Josiah Belden had left a sweetheart behind. Bidwell and Dawson stared silently, longingly into the fire, and George Shotwell left off his shyness and began softly and earnestly to speak with Lindy Gray.

All that day and into the night, Nancy recalled her own wedding. Visions of it stood out so clearly, then faded away again; one moment it seemed that the past was upon her, then again it seemed far, far away. Less than two years ago, it was like a whole lifetime. She wanted to talk about it, but Ben was tired. Softly she approached it.

"I'm proud you offered Isaac and Jessica our wagon for their wedding night."

"Did you clean it up some?" Ben asked.

"Of course I did!" Nancy retorted. Then softly, almost shyly, she asked, "Remember our weddin'? Remember the cakes?"

"Umm."

"And how Jimmy Brewster played his harmonica?"

"Like to make the roosters crow."

"Oh, come on. It was nice. Wasn't it, Ben? Wasn't it a nice wedding?"

"Umm."

Her heart began to pound, and her cheeks felt hot. There were questions needing to be asked, answers she ached to have. But she sighed and blew out the lantern and lay very still, to make the questions go away. Still, they were wound into her dreams, popping up in her thoughts like snakes in the grass, and the next morning began badly.

10

★★★

An evil smell hung in the air. Indian fires. In dry weather, Fitzpatrick said, the Indians would burn the prairie grass. The hazy smoke stung Nancy's eyes, made her throat feel raw, and when the midday heat came out full, it was twice as oppressive.

Nancy's back ached, and her arms felt heavy. Clouds of tiny black gnats had risen from the smoke. They billowed and buzzed around her head, trying to enter her eyes, mouth, and nose. Ann screamed and kicked as they stung, and at last, beside herself, Nancy gave the baby a slap on the leg and immediately reproached herself as a monster.

The smoke, the heat, the bugs made everyone irritable. From far off Nancy heard the Reverend Williams raise his voice in a heated reproach to one of the missionaries. They had been arguing for hours. Nancy's head began to throb as if she herself were involved. She had wrapped her shawl around her head against the insects, and now she felt she would die from the heat.

They camped at nooning without any water, and at night there was only a trickle from a nearly dry creek.

The plains began to change. Tall grass gave way to short, stubby grass. But the change was so gradual that it made time itself seem different. A day on the prairie could seem forever. All days were nearly the same, with nothing to mark their progress except for Fitzpatrick's call, "Twenty miles-o, a good day's ride."

They'd been out just a month, and Nancy could see changes. The travelers no longer asked so many questions of the guide, or seemed to care about the route, except to anticipate each night's encampment and sleep.

All along the North Platte, great herds of buffalo had been there for the taking. Now, as they came to the short grass, the herds dwindled. It caught them unaware. Even the captain said it was unusual for the herds to thin out so suddenly.

"We wasted the meat while there was plenty," muttered John Bidwell. He had shown his disgust from the start at men who killed buffalo only for the robes, ate only the tongue and brain, and left the rest of the meat to rot.

Nobody asked the question outright, but it nagged at Nancy. When the buffalo were all gone, what would they eat? How could seventy people subsist on a few bony jackrabbits and prairie dogs?

That night they ate strips of buffalo they'd jerked some days earlier, and a pickle each. Even the pickle barrel was over half-empty. Nancy had never realized the spicy tartness would taste so good out on the dry plains.

It was that night the luck began to run bad, as her pa would have said, with bad news coming in threes. The first was the disappearance of Lord Romain.

"Didn't ask no leave," said John Gray bitterly. He wiped his weathered face with a large, dirty bandana. His small dark eyes were always moist. "Just took off alone, after buffalo, the young fool. Like to kill himself, showin' off."

"Was he mounted?" Ben asked sharply.

"His horse is gone," replied Gray.

Nancy caught Ben's expression. "What's wrong?"

"Nothing. Nothing a'tall."

"Ben, there's something!" she said sharply.

"I'm going after him!" Ben burst out suddenly, ready to take Lightning and start off, but John Gray stood squarely before him.

"You're going no place," he declared, "with that young wife of your'n and a baby! Get yourself killed and leave her to fend for herself? Crazy fellow, crazy as the rest of 'em."

Another moment, and words would have led to blows, but Captain Fitzpatrick appeared and began to give orders. "Turn in those wagons! Gray, you can go and hunt your man. It's what he's paid you for, isn't it? Ben Kelsey, it's your watch tonight, from dark to midnight. I put Hooper, Belden, and Cook with you." He turned, sniffing the air as if to know from the smell what danger might come with the night. "This here is Pawnee country. They'll steal your horses and kill you anyhow, just for fun."

"Ben." Nancy touched his arm, wondering why his mouth was set that way and his shoulders stooped like a man much older. "What is it?"

"Andy. It was Andy made Romain bolt off like that. Andy fightin' with him yesterday, accusing him of stealing his tobacco."

"But Romain wouldn't . . . he's got his own things, and money."

"Well, you know Andy. Called Romain a coward. So Romain took off, the way I figure it, to prove he isn't."

"But where's Andy?"

Ben almost smiled. "He walked on back, damn fool, after I told him Romain wouldn't ever take his fool tobacco. I told Andy he probably dropped it himself. Never figured he'd go back twenty miles looking for it!"

"Well, Andy's right smart about tracking," Nancy said, making her voice gentle, though she felt an icy chill at the thought of Andy out alone. He was hard to live with and always ready to fight, but he was a Kelsey, after all, and Ben's youngest brother.

"I'm more worried about Romain," Ben said, then set out at Fitzpatrick's call for first watch.

It did no good to fret and worry about others. Nancy knew that. People had to take care of themselves in this world, and a worrying woman was no help. Still, thoughts of Andy and Romain followed her through her dreams, dreams of the pursuing Pawnee riding hot and hard, wanting first the white man's horse, then his blood. She'd heard the men telling of Pawnee sacrifices, how they'd tortured and butchered a fifteen-year-old girl, a Sioux captive. Father De Smet had told it; it had to be true.

By next afternoon Andy was back. He came in limping and sunken-eyed tired. Still, he gave Ben that crooked, cocky grin of his and boasted, "Found my tobaccy! Musta fallen out of my pocket around the fire that night. Saw a redskin poking around our campsite," he added casually. "Was about to shoot him, but he lit out."

Ben only shook his head helplessly, and Andy called back over his shoulder, "That idiot Romain get back yet?"

"Not yet."

All that day Romain was still missing, and the Reverend Williams was starting to leaf through his book, and Nancy saw him go off to a spot behind his wagon, seeming to practice words, for his head was thrown back and his eyes closed as in a sermon.

Late, late that night the horses began to whinny, and the men on watch grasped their rifles, and then the word rustled through their camp that Lord Romain had been found. In her sleep Nancy turned over with a sigh. Safe after all. Now, now it was over. But even before sunrise the second blow fell. It was Sam, come to wake them while the others still slept, his large bulk covering the entrance to their tent, his hands moving fretfully.

"It's Luke," he said hoarsely. "Been up-chuckin' all night. Got the cramps real bad."

Nancy leapt up, crashing into the cradle in her haste, hitting her leg a painful knock. "Fever?"

"I reckon."

"High?"

"Sadie said to get you."

"Now, Sam, you know we can't . . ." Ben, wide awake, had lit the lantern, and now he squatted down beside it, and his face was spotted with eerie shadows. "We've got our own babe to think about."

"Don't I know that, Ben?" Sam squatted down beside him, twisting his hands. "I don't mean for you to get near Luke. Just thought you could take the other kids. The babies. Keep 'em away from Luke, just in case . . ."

"Of course we will!" Nancy broke in quickly. In her mind, like a swiftly turning wheel the thought revolved, and she forced the word away. "Of course we'll watch them," she repeated, and quickly she pinned up a stray mass of hair and threw on her heavy cloak—quickly, to keep him from even saying the dreaded word or letting the awful thought come out into the open.

"I'll come on back with you and get them," she said.

"Nancy!" There was a hardness in Ben's voice.

She did not look back at Ben, but pretended not to have heard him, or to have misunderstood. "I'll be right back," she called, and went off into the darkness with Sam, trying in vain to think of something to say—anything, anything, that did not include the dreaded word *cholera.*

If it were the cholera—and all day the word rattled and rang in her brain like a pebble in a whirlpool—if it really was the cholera, why then, then they were doomed. Cholera was like rot; it was like a runaway fire; it was like sin. You had to cut it off, choke it out, kill it. You had to show no speck of mercy, or it moved in upon you. It wiped out cities and towns and villages—it could wipe out a wagon train down to every last man, woman, and child, and do it in a matter of days.

All that day Nancy sternly kept her mind on tending the two small boys. All day there was silence between her and Ben, even at nooning, and at night he took watch again. At dusk, when Jessica came to talk, Nancy asked her to mind the children.

"Of course I will, Nancy," Jessica said, without questions, and Nancy gratefully set out. It was good to be alone, even just a short distance away from the others.

She went to Lightning where he was hobbled, and she released him, so that he came of his own accord to nuzzle her shoulder and then her hand. Nancy laid her head against his neck, feeling the warmth, smelling the hide and sweat and fresh grassy smell of the horse.

"He thinks I'm crazy to take those kids," she whispered, close to Lightning's ear. "What could I do? Sadie can keep it quiet for a while, maybe another day or two. Then everyone will know. They'll find out about Luke, and then..." She paused, and the horse bobbed his head up and down. His large eyes were velvet-soft and knowing. "Then they'll cut them off. They'll leave them here in the middle of nowhere, just like they left the Williamses when Jessica was hurt, only now it's worse." She closed her eyes against the ache that flowed over her whole body. She dared not think of the rest of it.

How long could they keep Luke's illness a secret? A man like Fitzpatrick could sniff out such things. If it really was the... the cholera or ague, others would soon sicken and then...

She walked, leading Lightning with her hand on his neck, toward a small copse of aspen, spindly and frail, their leaves trembling in the prairie breeze. Wearily Nancy sat down, allowing Lightning to forage, mindful of the deeping dusk, yet needing to be apart from the others. She leaned back, inhaling deeply the fragrance of trees, which, among the grass, had become a rare treat. Glancing up, she saw the long, flat leaf of a willow, or a tree very like a willow, and she leapt to her feet.

Hastily she searched on the ground for a twig or stone. Finding none, she began to scratch at the bark with her fingernails, until she could peel away strips of it. Then, with a single leap, she mounted Lightning, even without a saddle or reins, and hurried back to camp, to Sadie's wagon.

Inside lay Luke on a bed of blankets, his little face fever-red and contorted. Sadie sat beside him, slumped over.

Startled, she gasped out, "Nancy! What are you doing here? Are the babies . . . ?"

"They're fine," Nancy said. She held out her hand with the strips of sticky, dirty bark with the sharp medicine smell.

"Give him some of this," she said. "Make him eat it. Give it to him with water. It might take down the fever. I recollect, my grandma used to use willow bark."

Sadie stared at her and opened her mouth into a full, round circle. "I declare. You came into this here wagon to give me . . . to bring Luke . . ."

"If none of us came into this wagon," Nancy said evenly, "it would look strange. It would look as if the Kelseys had something to hide."

Sadie could only stare at her for a long moment. Then she handed Nancy a tin cup, and Nancy scraped the bark and moisture from her palm into it.

"Sadie!" Nancy called back. "I'm not sure it will work." Then, before Sadie could respond, she was off into the night, to her own wagon.

Jessica was gone. In her place was Ben, his face swollen in anger. He had seen her going to Sadie's wagon. He only stared at her. If he'd threatened her or yelled, it would have been better than his terrible, accusing silence.

The silence said more than words. It confronted her. How could you do that? it said. How could you take a chance on bringing that sickness to Ann? To all of us? Pride, it said, makes you do these things. Pride makes you think you can cure anyone, when all you have is a handful of tree bark. Contrariness makes you go where you don't belong, makes you more stubborn than a mule, makes you put everyone in danger.

Ben turned and was gone, gone toward Bartleson's camp-fire, and Nancy was left alone, trembling. She looked down at Ann, half afraid even to touch her. Suppose that something of the sickness were clinging to her own hands?

All night she lay wakeful, supposing the worst that might still happen. The next day Luke was no better. And that afternoon the third stroke of evil was upon them. George Shotwell, getting out of his wagon just after nooning, ac-cidentally shot himself in the side. He was laid in the shade, and Captain Fitzpatrick came for Nancy, but she had nothing, nothing to help a dying man.

Now Nancy lay out under the stars with the cradle nearby and Ben out on watch. He had volunteered to go again, and Nancy was alone listening to the long, lonely night sounds, dazed and amazed at the words that kept rolling through her thoughts—no-return, no-return, no-return trail.

She was here, almost as if she'd been blown here like a seed or a feather, suddenly and without plan. Had she ever said she wanted to go west? Had she ever, even for a minute, agreed to this sort of life?

She sighed heavily. Maybe, she thought, turning to see the farthest star on the horizon, maybe she had agreed. Maybe it was something more than words that said yes or no. Thoughts circled in her head, but again she could not grasp them. Al-ways it was like this, with the new idea hanging just at the edge of her mind, yet always beyond reach. If she had time to think, to let it all settle, time to get the right words to-gether . . .

She gave a start as footsteps rustled near her. She knew at once that it was Ben. Ben, come to rail at her, most likely. She closed her eyes tightly. She didn't want to hear it. He was not pleased. She had not pleased him. It was the only thing Ma had told her about husbands and wives, the only thing she was supposed to remember. "Be pleasing to your husband, Nancy. You must make yourself pleasing to him in all ways."

☆ **80** ☆

Inside her a pounding felt like drums, rising, until she could bear it no longer, and she sat bolt upright, her fists clenched and jaw firm. Without warning she turned on him.

"Ben Kelsey!" She hissed out his name and would have shouted were it not for the night. "Ben Kelsey, don't you sit there watching me, thinking bad while I sleep, like to put some hex on me! I did nothing wrong but try to cure Luke if I could, and if that's wrong, well, it's just as wrong to take a body away from their own homestead and out in the middle of a desert where people shoot themselves and die, and people . . ."

Ben came close, his head bent down nearly touching hers. "I came to tell you," he said, his voice deep, but hushed, "I came to tell you Luke's mendin'. The fever broke."

11

In her first flush of gratitude, Nancy did not question it. Luke was better. That was all that mattered. Then she began to wonder. The thought persisted, as stubborn as a saddle burr: How could he have gotten better so fast? Cholera didn't get cured in three days! Was it the willow bark? Was it really cholera? If so, how come nobody else caught it? And then— could it be that willow was a cure for it?

She did not want to question Sadie. Sadie was grateful and at peace, on the Reverend Williams's advice, thanking the Lord for a miracle.

Quite by accident Nancy discovered the truth. They had turned in early one afternoon late in June. Classens, the blacksmith with the missionaries, had promised to help all the men with the shoeing of horses and oxen.

While the men were busy, the women tended to washing, and Nancy brought Ann to the edge of a little creek, deter-mined to scrub the dust and vermin out of the baby's hair. No sooner had she finished and wrapped Ann in her shawl, than she came upon Billy, Luke, and Mary sitting in a semi-circle with their legs folded Indian style, playing at pow-wow. Their little faces were streaked with mud, and they had tucked bird feathers into their hair. They were passing a stone around, pretending to suck on it as on a pipe.

Nancy glanced at them and smiled. She heard Mary say, "We should find some of those *pitty* flowers. Make a better pipe. Those *pitty* flowers, like a bell."

"Where did you find them?" asked Billy, gazing around.

"Way back," replied Mary. "Back the day Luke got sick. I never got to try, because my mother called me."

For a moment Nancy walked on. Then she burst upon the children so forcibly that Mary immediately began to cry. "What flowers?" she demanded. "Foxglove? Luke, was it foxglove?"

She knelt down beside him, struggling to remain calm. "Please tell me, Luke. Did you put that flower into your mouth?"

Luke squirmed uneasily, and his face went beet-red.

"You can tell me, Luke," Nancy whispered, coaxing. "I won't get you into trouble with your ma, I promise. Was it a flower about so big, yellow and white, shaped like a very long bell?"

Slowly Luke nodded, his eyes shut tight.

"Did you eat any?"

"Little bit."

Nancy sat back on her heels, and with a great sigh she took Luke's hands into hers. "Honey, you didn't know better, but that was an awful mistake. You could have died. Foxglove is poison. That's what made you so sick. If you'd had more of it . . ."

Nancy stood up, and she made the other children stand near, so that she could look into their faces. "Never," she said sternly, "never put anything into your mouth that you find in the fields or the woods. Lots of plants are poisonous. You could die."

"But, Aunt Nancy," Billy ventured, twisting his hands, "*you* use plants for tea and tonics."

"That's different!" Nancy cried. "You can't just use any plants. Some are medicine, and some are poison. You have to learn to tell the difference. A little bit of lobelia tea can cure a person. But too much could kill them. I want you kids never, never to eat anything unless your folks give it to you. Understand?"

Solemnly they nodded and promised. Walking back with them, Nancy felt sober and stunned. There was so much one must teach a child. Oh, how watchful one had to be! There were so many dangers everywhere, and the children always into something else. How much simpler it would be to raise them back home in the cabin, where all the neighbors were friends, where no wild Indians roamed and the kids were kept close by, tending their chores. Well, at least in California they'd all have each other. Just as she'd looked after these children, Sadie, Lindy, and Jessica would help her with Ann and with others yet to be born.

As they walked, Billy asked to hold his little cousin, and Ann's face bobbed over his shoulder and she laughed aloud and cooed. A warm, good feeling came over Nancy. It was good to have one another!

Nancy and Ben were nearly at the end of the train, and Indian fires had added a thick smoky haze to the rising dust, so that when the monuments came into view, Nancy blinked and rubbed her eyes, doubting her vision.

Like reddish-brown hills in the distance, the forms soon grew longer and sharper, as if a hand were chiseling them out even as she watched. Nancy stopped in her tracks to stare. A strange shiver prickled at the back of her neck, though the day was blazing hot. A thrusting ache rose in the pit of her stomach, and she stood open-mouthed.

Ben too had stopped. He left the oxen in their tracks, and together he and Nancy moved toward the wondrous shapes.

"Ben!" she breathed. "What is it? It's so—so beautiful."

"It's—a pile of rocks," Ben said.

Bidwell and Jimmy-John rode back toward them, having been sent to bring up the rear. "Fitzpatrick says get ready to turn in."

"Those rocks . . ." Ben pointed.

"Courthouse Rocks, they call 'em," said Bidwell. "The priest says they're called that because they resemble buildings.

He says they look like castles he's seen in the south of France."

Nancy turned to ask, "Can we go there?"

"No." Bidwell shook his head. "Fitzpatrick says the place is crawling with rattlesnakes and other poisonous reptiles. It's beautiful, isn't it?"

While Jimmy-John rode on down the trail, Bidwell remained for several minutes, looking out to the formations, and then Nancy heard him quote softly,

> "Enough of Science and of Art;
> Close up those barren leaves;
> Come forth, and bring with you a heart
> That watches and receives."

For a long moment the silence seemed so great that Nancy could feel the slightest stirring of her own breath. She longed to hear the words once more, to understand their full meaning. But she did not ask Bidwell to repeat them. *Bring with you a heart that watches . . .*

When Bidwell left them, Ben turned to Nancy. There was a distant look on his face as he gazed far, far beyond the formations. "Just seeing it," he said softly, "is enough. We don't have to go and be there. I reckon I'll remember it for always. And everything we've seen. Even the bad parts, like the stampede and the river crossings and the freezing rain, I'll remember it all when I'm old. Some folks never hardly see anything. My pa never saw anything more'n the Ohio River. Well, his boys are going to see the Pacific! That's a lot. A lot to remember when you're old."

Nancy only nodded in silence. Ben's eyes were so very dark and bright, his features smooth, yet firm. A feeling leapt up in her, as if she and Ben had been apart for many weeks and she had missed him sorely.

They camped that night and the next in sight of Courthouse Rocks and Chimney Rock, which, true to its name, looked like a gigantic smokestack. The formations seemed somehow like living things raised up in the middle of nowhere. The sight seemed to bring consolation to the travelers. Everyone spoke more quietly. There was a settled-down feeling, and when Nancy asked Ben how these fantastic shapes had been created, he replied unexpectedly, with awe in his voice, "The hand of God, Nancy."

Next they passed within sight of Scott's Bluff, a smoky-blue butte rising up out of the prairie, and the story was whispered from one man to the next, told to Nancy and Ben by Cheyenne Dawson.

"Like a tale out of a book," Dawson said, and he told of a trapper named Hiram Scott. "He and Sublette, Bridger and Fitzpatrick went out together. Scott got sick, so they camped at Laramie's Fork. But all their powder had gotten wet in a canoe accident, so they couldn't hunt. They tried looking for fruits and roots, waiting for Scott to get better. Well"— Dawson took a deep breath—"Scott just got weaker, and they couldn't find any food, so they decided to leave him. They told Scott they were just going out to look for food. What they were really doing was trying to track a party of hunters who'd left a fresh trail and get back to the fort."

Dawson made a wry face. "They caught up with the hunters, all right. They told them Scott was dead. That was in autumn, 1828. The next spring they found Scott's skeleton. Scott had walked sixty miles from where they'd abandoned him, and he died right there, at the foot of the bluff. They named it for him."

Dawson scratched his head. "It's hard to figure. Here's Fitzpatrick. We all know him. He takes care of those missionaries and this whole train. But—back then—he left a man out here to die. It's hard to figure how the same man can be two different ways."

"Seems to me," Ben said, "all men are two different ways."

Nick gave a startled look. "That's so, Ben," he said. "I never thought of it that way."

Beyond the landmarks, a rugged path led to Fort Laramie.

When at last they arrived, the sight of the high wooden towers made Nancy's eyes sting with sudden emotion. One could grow lonely, she realized, for wooden walls, chimneys, chairs, and store goods. Inside, the wares nearly took her breath away. She and the other women stood close together, marveling as if they had never before seen such things as blankets, hatchets, hammers, cloth, pots, and spoons.

"How'd all this get here?" Jessica breathed.

"The prices!" exclaimed Lindy. "Fifteen dollars for a blanket!"

"I declare, a dollar for a cup of sugar," said Sadie. "It's outrageous."

But the biggest wonder was out in the courtyard, where two Indian tepees stood, with Indian children playing about and their mothers cooking corn cakes over their fires. The sight made Nancy and the other women rush back to the trading post, their eyes wide, questions bursting inside them.

Watching them from among several barrels of beans and sugar, half leaning on the counter, stood a lean, firm-jawed man in trapper's clothes. He had but one eye. The other was covered with a patch. He straightened himself to full height, then walked a few steps toward Sadie, but looking all the while at Lindy.

"I'd be pleased to show you ladies around the fort," he said. His words were addressed to Sadie, but his smile was for Lindy.

"I'm Richard Phelan," he added, "an old friend of Captain Fitzpatrick. If you have any questions about the fort . . ."

Sadie was bursting with impatience. "We all wonder," she asked, "how come there's Injuns camped in the courtyard. We thought this fort was to protect white trappers from the redskins."

"Well, I surely can understand your puzzlement, then," Phelan said. "But those Indian squaws are wives of some of the trappers." He was silent for a moment. Then, for the first time, he looked fully at Lindy Gray. "It gets terrible lonesome out here in the mountains," he said. "So lonesome a man can lose his mind."

He kept his gaze on Lindy, steady and without smiling. In the same way she returned his look.

For two days they rested within the walls of Fort Laramie. When they moved out again, Richard Phelan was with them, off to see the coast, he said, but everyone knew better.

Day by day the prairie flattened out even more, with high peaks to taunt them always far, far in the distance, and the land now covered with the hard, dry-smelling sagebrush, with not even a sapling remaining.

At the beginning of the journey, for the first week or so, every day had stood out in Nancy's mind. She reckoned that even now she could remember every single detail of the first week on the trail. Then, strangely, time began to move forward in larger measures, so that she could hardly distinguish the third week from the fourth. Now that they'd been out two months, the entire trek seemed like an endless succession of freezing nights and dragged-out days, rushing to pack and eat, then walking, walking, walking, one more step, one more, one more, looking forward to a bit of shade, a sip of water, some hot food, and the sleep that never lasted quite long enough.

Sagebrush scraped at their legs and arms. It worried the horses, the tough fibers sticking in their mouths. It made a crackling, harsh-smelling fuel, the only available fuel at all.

There was not much to cook with it. The men hunted for black-tailed rabbits. Sometimes a badger was dug up from its hole and stewed in a pot into an evil-tasting soup. It took half a dozen prairie dogs to make a decent pot pie for three people, and the meat on those bones was tough pickings. If only they'd brought a cow! More and more Nancy wished for it. She took a tuck in her skirt.

With hunger, tempers were hotter. Vicious fights began over nothing and lasted for days. Even Talbot Green, usually so polite, sank his fist into Belden's face one day, snarling, "Stay out of my wagon, you hear? Stay away from my goods! If I catch you poking around my things, I swear, I'll cut your heart out, you low-down, vermin-ridden . . ."

"Whatever in hell's so important in that junk of yours?" shouted Belden. "Just rags and dung . . ."

"Stay away from my things!"

And one night late in July, old John Gray and his pleasure seekers—Amos Frye, Romain, and a few others—announced they were turning back. "Nothing much to stay for," Gray said. "Hunting's nothing to brag about from here on in. We've seen the sights."

They had engraved their names on the surface of Independence Rock, along with most of the other travelers. "That's what I set forth to do," said Romain, "and shoot buffalo and sight the Rocky Mountains." He seemed well satisfied with his trophies.

There were no real good-byes, just a nod. "See ya. S'long."

The next day they were gone, and Nancy felt a strange pang at the thought that some could really turn back and go home. Home, for her, was a wagon now, and a tent.

Somehow, with their sportsmen gone, it all seemed more earnest. A weariness had set in that they could not dispel, even when Father De Smet performed the marriage ceremony for Richard Phelan and Lindy Gray.

It was not like the other wedding. Lindy was pale and quiet. Little Mary stood by with a basket of wildflowers, not knowing whether to smile or cry. The men tried to bluster and laugh as before, but it was different now. They'd come about halfway to California. And something in the set of Fitzpatrick's jaw, in the sober sighs of Father De Smet, in the hurried departure of John Gray, told them that the first half of the trip had been too easy.

12

★★★

On August 10, midmorning, they arrived at Soda Springs, and even Jimmy-John sat down alone and very quiet, his journal book on his knee, looking about now and then as he wrote down the wonders before him.

Everything combined at Soda Springs to make up for the long, dry, drab days of the past months. Where before there had been only dust, now there were pools of water amid cool rocks. Where everything had been flat, now tall trees stretched up and up, giving shade, giving the smell of greenery. Now there was the cascading rush of water spilling down the high ridges and bubbling up in small geysers.

Everybody bathed in the clear, cool water. Nancy took Ann and washed her completely, dusted her with fine alkali powder, combed her soft hair into curls. She was sitting up now, clapping her hands gleefully, laughing at anything that pleased her—a shiny pebble, a bird, a flower.

Nancy had never seen a place so beautiful. And yet, it seemed familiar, as if she had felt this way before, smelled the same trees of fir and cedar, felt the same cool water lapping at her body, tasted the same richness of good water, and felt healed.

Everyone felt the miracle of the place. The men drank the waters as if they were tonic. The priests washed their dusty robes. Jessica became quiet, contemplating the beauty. Lindy's color returned, and she laughed with Mary and splashed in the pool and lay back at last with a great sigh and a smile. "It should be like this. I mean, life should have more times like this. Why does it always have to be so hard?"

"Maybe we make it hard," Jessica said.

"We don't make it hard," argued Sadie, wringing out a shirt. "It just is plain hard, and that's the will of the Lord."

"Well, if a person sees two trails," said Lindy, "he doesn't always have to take the steep one, does he?"

Sadie laughed harshly. "No indeed! But you go telling that to a stubborn ox like my Sam!"

Nancy, intent on gathering pine cones for a fire, stopped short. Something in Sadie's tone told more than words. She felt a unity between the two women, a certain tension they shared.

"What about Sam?" Nancy spoke loudly, and her voice made them all turn. "What do you mean, Sadie?"

"Mean about what?" Sadie pursed her lips tightly. "I'm not meaning anything—just Sam's stubborn. You know that, Nancy."

"Well, I guess all the Kelseys are stubborn," put in Jessica, laughing lightly.

Determinedly, Nancy shrugged off the uneasy feeling. It was as if they all knew something she didn't, as if they had all made a plan and were keeping it to themselves, the way grownups keep things from children.

Ben would have chided her, "Don't be so thin-skinned, Nancy! Always imagining things."

But the more Nancy tried to push aside her uneasiness, the more it festered. What would Sadie and Lindy possibly have to hide from her?

Things were said—remarks without clear meaning in themselves, but later, when Nancy recalled them, they all fit together. It was like the same idea hitting lots of different people all at once, far back in their minds where they hadn't put it into words yet, but it made them talk in riddles and about concerns that didn't quite touch on the true worry. The real worry still lay too deep, too far away to be recognized.

Things were said: "This ox of mine is pretty near dead. Don't see how he can go another mile."

"See this toe of mine? It's full of pus."

"My missus says she feels like she's walked a million miles."

"Flour's running out. Can't stand meat without bread."

"I hear we're like to have an early winter. Sometimes it does snow in the mountains in September."

"Let's see that map again. You sure this here's right?"

For two days they hemmed and hawed and circled around it. Nobody wanted to be the first to say it. Once you called a thing, you were stuck with it.

On the third afternoon at Soda Springs, Nancy and Jessica went berrying, with Sadie minding Ann. They planned to bake a cake, using the soda water to make it rise.

"Captain Fitzpatrick says it'll work fine," Jessica rambled. "He says some of the men drink gallons of it, like beer, and actually get drunk! Of course, it's just in their minds. Did you know, Mr. Bartleson sold a whole cartful of whiskey to those trappers a while back? He brought it along on purpose, to sell. Isaac says they all *swore* to leave whiskey behind, and nobody minded so much when some of the men just took a swallow or two, but imagine, a whole cartful, after he swore! Isaac says he can't stand the sight of that Bartleson anymore. Isaac says he's two-faced, always laughing and jolly and acting like he's everybody's friend when he's really just out for his own skin and his own belly. Did you see all he ate of that deer they caught? Isaac says he'd never follow a man like that, and . . ."

She stopped abruptly and sat down under the shade of three tall pine trees, and Nancy sat down, too. They looked out to the distant mountains, snow-topped even in summer. Then Nancy looked at Jessica. Her face was flushed and damp, and her eyes had that swollen look. She looked at Jessica, at the mountains, at Jessica, and then she said dully, "You're not going on to California with us, are you."

Jessica said nothing, but her chest heaved as she breathed

hard, her lips parted, and she stared straight down at a spot on the ground. Then she shook her head. "We're going to Oregon instead. We're going with the guide. Nancy," she said without warning, "I'm pregnant."

It seemed as if a stone had lodged in Nancy's throat. She did not move or speak or feel anything, only that a stone was cutting off her breath, her voice.

Pregnant? She repeated the word to herself. *Pregnant?* Neither she nor her mother nor any of her kin used that word. They'd say, "I'm carrying," or "with child," or "that way."

Thoughts tumbled about her, like the rushing of the waterfall. Jessica—a mother—then she'd be an aunt. There'd be another cousin for Ann.

Nancy gazed at Jessica. Then she asked, "You feeling poorly?"

"Yes."

"Now?"

"All the time, I reckon."

Nancy sighed. Yes, she knew.

"It's crazy for us to think of going to California," Jessica said. "Even if I ride in the wagon. Isaac's worried about me."

"And your folks?" Nancy asked dully, though she knew, she already knew by Jessica's face.

"My folks want to settle in Oregon, too. They've been thinking it for a long time. Makes sense to go along with Captain Fitzpatrick, to settle near the missionaries. It's safe in Oregon, and some other white people are there, some Americans. Anyhow, there's a trail—a real trail."

Nancy nodded. She felt cold, as if with fever, that kind of hot-cold chill. She said, "It will seem like we're cut in half. You and Isaac in Oregon. Sadie and Lindy and me in California."

"Sadie wants to go to Oregon, too," said Jessica. "And Lindy."

"And Lindy? All of you? *All the women?*"

Nancy's eyes widened, and her hands pressed down on the

ground beneath her, as on the night of the terrible stampede, when the earth shook. A strange notion came into her head, of her bonnet lying in its store-bought wrapping papers in the wagon. What difference did a bonnet make without any kin around? She wanted to scream it out, realizing the senselessness of the thought, but she couldn't rid herself of the notion of the bonnet, the bonnet, the beautiful bonnet ready to wear to meeting, to outings, to picnics, to town. In all her imaginings, she had included the others, the clan of Kelseys, the travelers she had come to know.

Numb, Nancy shook her head. She stood up. "And Sam? Is Sam willing to give up the idea of going to California?"

Jessica shrugged. Tears slid down her cheeks, endlessly, yet her face was not changed by them. "You know Sadie. She'll get her way."

Luke! Luke and Billy and Jeremy and the two babies she'd tended—they would be gone to Oregon, gone, for all the difference it would make, from the face of the earth. She'd never see them again. Oh, likely when they were grown, maybe then. But all the growing years, the questions and plans and changing. She'd miss that. Oh, God, how she'd miss that.

Still, tears slid down Jessica's cheeks, and again the stone clung tight in Nancy's throat, and she leaned toward her friend, wanting to open her heart and cry until she was done. But gently she put her arms around Jessica. She drew her up. She kissed her lightly on the cheek and she said, "Jessica! For Lord's sake, you mustn't cry. Don't you know it dries up your milk?"

Jessica sniffed and smiled in spite of herself. "What milk, you silly!"

"Come on!" Nancy said fiercely, her eyes blazing. "Come on, now! We're going to gather berries, buckets full of berries, and we're going to have that cake tonight!"

She began to run up the hillsides, crookedly like the mountain sheep, rushing ahead, grasping at the thornberry bushes, stripping the berries into her bucket so swiftly that the thorns bit into her fingers and they bled. Still she ran, stumbling and scrambling between the rocks, higher, higher, until she could look down at Jessica below, the red hair standing out all frizzy, the blue eyes troubled, puzzled, wide.

At last she came down, and quietly they walked back to camp, made their cakes, baked them, and offered them to the children.

It was after supper, with the pans put away and Ann tucked into her cradle, that Ben came to sit a spell by the fire, and he began to whittle at a stick he had, watching the chips fall around his feet.

Then Nancy said, "Well, Ben."

And he said, "You heard. Some of them are going to Oregon instead."

"Yes." Nancy was grateful for the dark.

"Sam says it's better for the boys. Sadie doesn't want to raise them in the wilderness. The preacher's going to Oregon, too."

"Yes."

"Fitzpatrick's going to guide them all the way there. It's a good trail. Missionaries have used it half a dozen times before. There's a fort on the way. They'll be home in a month."

"That'll be nice."

For a time there was silence, except for the snapping of the pine cones burning in their small fire and the dull sound of Ben's chips hitting the ground.

"Those pine cones sure do burn fine." Nancy felt as if she were split into two people, one just watching, the other deciding. "Look, Ben," she said, "they blaze up in colors. Guess there's lots of pine in California."

Ben whittled five more strokes, then two more. "Pine in Oregon too, I guess." He seemed not to be breathing at all.

"But in Oregon," Nancy said, her heart pounding, "there's no oranges growing. There's no wild horses to be had, free. Maybe you can't even walk down to the Pacific Ocean!"

The last she said with a violence, though her voice was low, and she stood up and walked to the fire, stared down at the bursting pine cones, then turned back to Ben. He had risen, too, and let the knife fall.

"Nancy!" He held her. "Are you sure?"

"Of course I'm sure! We set out to go to Californ-y. Now, how we going to get to Californ-y if we give up midway? How are we ever going to know what it's really like?"

"Nancy!" It was a whisper so glad, so filled with amazement, that Nancy put her finger to his lips.

"Hush, Ben. You'll wake the whole world. We'd better turn in. I guess we'll be starting in the morning."

13

The next morning they pulled up their stakes in greater haste than usual. Perhaps Fitzpatrick planned it that way. Long good-byes were hard on everyone. Those California-bound, thirty men and Nancy and Ann, stood together, forming their own small band. Andy, at the last moment, decided to push on to California, too, and Nancy was surprised at her own happiness at having another Kelsey along.

"Catch up! Catch up! Catch up!" Fitzpatrick raised his hand high in the unforgettable signal.

The men shuffled their feet. The brothers were awkward with each other. "Well, Isaac. Good luck. Take care of those boys, Sam, you hear? You come on out to Californ-y and visit."

"Sure, sure."

"Jessica." Nancy held out the box from the store back in Weston. "Jessica, this here's for you."

"Your bonnet? Nancy, I couldn't."

"You take it! Please, Jessica. I'd be proud to have you wear it when you take your first-born to church."

Wordlessly Jessica took the bonnet, then threw her arms around Nancy and kissed her, and she kissed Ben, too.

Sadie came bustling up, blinking rapidly, her round face flushed. She patted Nancy's arm again and again. Mrs. Williams gathered Nancy into her arms, pressed her against her stout bosom, then turned away, crying. Lindy whispered close to Nancy's ear, "Take care, dear. You and Ben will be just fine. You're strong."

Bartleson, wearing a wide-brimmed hat with a preposterous band of gold braid around it, barked orders, repeating Fitzpatrick's advice. "Patton and Jones! You go on to Fort Hall. Try to find that mountain man, Joel Walker. He's the only one that's been clear to California. Find him, and ask him if he'll guide us. The rest of us'll go on down the Bear River. We'll meet you at Cache Valley."

With only half their party left, Nancy felt exposed and nervous. There had been protection in numbers. And the presence of the missionaries had been reassuring. Now as they proceeded slowly along the Bear River, Nancy realized how often in a day, without even thinking of it, she had looked for Fitzpatrick and, sighting him, she'd breathed easier. Now Bartleson led, and the way was halting, uncertain. He sought trappers' tracks, sometimes forging recklessly ahead, while other times he stopped short so that horses and wagons nearly collided.

The first day they made only ten miles. Bartleson gave the order to turn in long before dusk. Bidwell and Jimmy-John glanced at each other and shrugged, and Nancy heard Jimmy-John mutter, "If he keeps up this snail's pace, I'm striking out alone."

The two brought out their fishing gear. "We'll catch you all some supper!" Jimmy-John called out. "You just get those fires started."

The day had turned stifling hot. Nancy, in no mood for a fire, gathered greens and berries near the river. Those with some of yesterday's biscuits and the last of the salt pork would do them for supper. But the others waited for the promised fish. As darkness fell they became uneasy, then angry.

"Those young fools!" shouted Bartleson. "Always going off on their own, no care for anyone but themselves! We wait supper for them, and they just forget about the rest of us."

Nick Dawson approached Bartleson hesitantly. "Maybe," he suggested, "they're lost."

"Lost?" Bartleson snickered. "Those two jackasses? Not

likely. They probably shot themselves a buck and decided to eat it all themselves. What do they care about the rest of us?"

Night settled in. Uneasiness changed to fear. Nobody spoke above a murmur. Fires were doused early. It felt wrong with so few of them, as if the night would swallow them up. The air vibrated with sounds. All night men got up and paced restlessly around the wagons, sat up a spell, then returned to their bedrolls to lie awake, tense.

"They're all thinking Bidwell and Jimmy-John have been killed by Indians," Nancy whispered to Ben. "Fitzpatrick said to look out for Blackfeet."

"They had rifles," said Ben.

"But maybe their powder got wet."

"At daybreak," he said, "Dawson and me and some others will go lookin' for them."

At noon the next day the searchers returned, shaking their heads. Bartleson decided instantly. "Move out!"

They had gone two hours when a commotion of shouts brought everything to a halt. "We've been to the snow!" Bidwell and Jimmy-John came racing, laughing. "Look! We brought back a hunk of snow for you all!"

Gleefully Bidwell opened his handkerchief. There lay a packed, muddy clump of ice, and Bartleson began to curse, his face puffed with rage. Even Nick Dawson exploded angrily.

"Snow!" he shouted. "You've been to the snow? Why, we thought you were *dead*. We sat up all night, imagining you'd been scalped. And you decide to go to the *snow* like a couple of idiots."

They retreated, meek and shame-faced as two schoolboys caught pranking. Later, exuberantly they told how they'd seen a snowy peak and, it being so hot, they decided to go there. They'd goaded each other on, with the snow mountain always just ahead, beyond reach. After midnight they'd arrived above the timberline, with the snow still above them.

"We had to sleep in a bear's lair," Jimmy-John said.

"In the morning," said Bidwell, "we just scrambled on up to the snow and scraped some off. I'm a mite tired now, I'll admit. But I've got a pocketful of grizzly hair for my trouble!" He showed it to Nancy, grinning.

"You could have been killed by that bear!" Nancy exclaimed.

"That's true."

"You might have been scalped by Indians."

"Yes."

"Or you could have gotten lost up in those mountains forever!"

John Bidwell leaned back with his hands behind his neck. "But what's the use of living at all," he pondered, "if you don't see the world around you? A person has to take some chances."

Nancy nodded. "I suppose."

"You yourself aren't taking the easy way," he said. "You could be safe and warm at Fort Hall this very minute."

Safe at Fort Hall with the others . . . Nancy tried not to think of it, but her mind continually returned to them. She kept seeing Jessica's red curls and Sam's big wagon with the huge canvas top and the mattress sticking out.

For the next week, their pace was a slow ten miles a day. To Nancy it seemed unreal, for she was like two separate selves, one moving ahead, the other hanging back.

Several times Ben asked her anxiously, "Are you all right?"

"What? Yes, yes." Then she would squint her eyes against the dense smoke of Indian fires and try to avoid the twisted sage as she walked. She led Lightning and placed Ann in the sling of her shawl, to have one hand free; she could brush away the biting flies and gnats.

Where was Cache Valley? They sent Andy to ride ahead. He reported only more brush, steep canyons, and crags.

Ben walked with his head down, alert for obstacles or tracks. Bartleson decided to bring up the rear. They had to stop constantly to fill in gullies or to bring out the ropes when a precipice was too steep for wagons and animals. Then there was always the grumbling and shouting.

Late one day Bartleson began to shout hysterically. "Water!" They had camped without any water for the last two nights. "See those trees up ahead?" he cried. "Look! We'll turn that way. Trees mean there's water nearby."

Ben, squinting to where Bartleson pointed, slowly shook his head. "I don't think so, Cap'n." He used the title; Bartleson insisted on it. "Sometimes at a distance the brush can fool you."

"I've got a keen eye, Ben Kelsey."

"I think it's a mirage."

"Damn it, man! You're not looking in the right place! I tell you, there's a whole clump of willows!"

Bartleson forced them on until the moon was high. Nancy, having given up on walking, rode Lightning, her head bobbing on her chest. A numbness had spread over her body. She had no feeling at all in her feet, no power to think straight. Visions kept washing over her, so that in her fatigue she could not tell whether she was awake or dreaming.

Her head suddenly jerked up as Lightning pawed the ground. In the moonlight shrubs and bushes were magnified; they loomed like the shapes of people, deep purple and black. It was icy cold, so that at first Nancy thought they stood on a plain of ice, and indeed, it was level as a floor and glistening white, beautiful and terrible, and Lightning's hooves crackled against it, and then wagon wheels began slowly, slowly to sink.

The oxen, exhausted from days of poor pasture and drought, made a final effort, then slumped down, their legs buckling under them.

To Nancy's dazed mind everything was happening so very slowly. She saw Ben stoop down to take a pinch of the crusty stuff in his hand. He touched his tongue to it, shook his head, and said grimly, "Salt. We've struck the salt flat. We must be near Salt Lake. Nancy!" He pulled her down from the horse, took Ann from her, and made her walk. She straightened her left arm, and she felt the same prickling, tingling as in her feet.

"Water?" She could hardly get the word out. Her tongue felt thick and warm.

"Here's some." Slowly Ben led her to a water hole, a muddy depression between clumps of sage brush.

"Where's Cache Valley?"

"We've passed it, sure," grumbled Colonel Chiles. "We're far south of our course."

Bartleson bent his great bulk down to fill his cup, drank, then spat. "Hellish brine!" he screamed. "This water's all salt. The devil take it!"

"You'd best drink some," Ben said calmly. "It'll keep you alive."

He offered Nancy a cup. "Drink it."

She did, and immediately began to feel sick. The salt-mineral taste made her gag.

"Keep that inside of you!" Ben ordered. "You'll dry up otherwise, Nancy. Just don't think of it. Here." He thrust a hard, dry biscuit at her. It had lain in his knapsack for at least three days, and tasted like a lump of clay. But Nancy chewed and chewed, forcing the heavy mass into a paste. Then she took half of it onto her finger and poked it into Ann's mouth. She felt the merest edge of a little tooth against her finger.

"I need more," she said, avoiding Ben's eyes.

"Don't you have some in your saddlebag?"

"No. I thought you did. I ate the last of mine this morning."

Quietly Ben said, "There's no more flour in the barrel."

Nancy still did not meet his eyes. Sugar had run out weeks ago, and beans and lard. Currants, dried apples, the jar of honey had long since been consumed.

She bent to dip the cup again into the brackish water. It did not satisfy her thirst, tasting worse than pickle juice, worse than ash. But she forced Ann's lips open and poured a bit of it into her mouth.

"She doesn't need water," Ben began.

"Yes, she does, Ben."

His features froze. "Nancy—don't you . . . ?"

"It's all right, Ben. I'll feed her what I eat. She doesn't really need milk anymore." Nancy's face felt flushed with the lie, and again the salty water threatened to rise from her rebellious stomach. She swallowed again and again. "She'll be all right, Ben."

"But I thought little babies needed—need milk for a long time, for a year or two."

"No," Nancy said stoutly. "Not always. Some babies never nurse but six months, and they're just fine." But then, they had milk from a cow or a goat, of course. Ann would have to learn to tolerate bits of tough sage hen and rabbit and the sharp mountain greens they sometimes found near the riverbanks. She would have to, or die. Already the little face was too thin, too delicate. Nancy could see the faint, bluish hollows beneath Ann's eyes.

She hurried to lay out their bedrolls, too weary to set up the tent. Nobody even bothered to hobble the animals; they were too exhausted to stray.

In the morning Lightning nuzzled the salty ground and lipped the brackish water, then leapt back, snorting. He tried to eat from a patch of grass between the bushes. It sparkled as if covered with frost. It was salt, and the horse refused to eat it, tossing his head, nostrils flaring.

For a whole day they laid by to rest the animals, hunting small game, but there was none.

The next day, when Bartleson signaled to move out toward the west, Ben shook his head. "No," he said firmly. "We'll get ourselves caught in the salt flats."

"Where then, Kelsey?" Hooper, Green, and Bidwell clustered around him.

"As I recollect we've got to head north, then west, to go around Salt Lake. We should hit the Green River."

"Catch up! Catch up!" cried Bartleson, pointing north. By sundown they reached the river, and there they rested for a week, waiting for their scouts to bring them the famous guide, Joel Walker.

But when the two scouts found them, they looked haggard and desperate. "No guide," they said. "Joel Walker wasn't there. We got directions, though. Folks at the fort said not to go too far south, or we'd get stuck in the salt flats."

"Do tell," said Ben.

"And not to go too far north, either, or we'll get stuck in terrible steep canyons. We have to go north-west."

"That's what I thought," put in Bartleson.

"Unless," added the scouts, "you want to turn back now to Fort Hall. We could still get a guide to Oregon, maybe even catch up with our party."

Talbot Green stepped forward. With a pointed stick he drew a circle in the dirt, while the others stood by, grave and silent. "Toss a pebble into this here circle if you want to go on to California," Green said. "We'll all close our eyes. No fighting, then. Majority rules."

"Maybe somebody will toss more than one pebble!" Andy objected.

"Grove Cook will watch," said Green with a nod.

Cook took his stance.

In the end, twenty-nine pebbles lay within the crude circle. On to California.

14

★★★

Now came the wild country. Cliffs rose up stark. Canyons plunged deep into rock piles. Trees grew gnarled and fierce between boulders; everything was tough and unyielding.

Nancy could see changes in Ben, and she wondered whether he saw them in her. He never mentioned her looks—never had, likely never would. And she had no mirror. But her fingertips showed her some changes.

As for Ben, his beard had become grizzled and tough. His eyes had gotten that same fiery brightness that she had seen in John Gray and Captain Fitzpatrick. Small lines were settling deeper around his eyes and on his brow. More and more, Ben's lips had that tight, set look, especially when he was around Bartleson. Ben never indicated by so much as a gesture the disgust he felt, but Nancy knew.

She knew, too, that he was worried about Ann. For a week or so Ann whimpered almost continually. Then she gave up and quieted down, and got thinner, living on the broths that Nancy boiled each night. She made broth from the carcass of a wild cat that Hooper caught, from the discarded feet and heads of two scrawny sage hens, from wild onions or mushrooms. The baby had learned to drink the broth from a cup.

More than once John Bidwell asked them, "You folks out of flour? I brought extra. Can't stand meat without bread. Maybe you could use some for the child?"

"Thanks," Ben said. "We can manage."

When September came, frost began to cover their bedrolls at night, and those who had wagons began to sleep in them. And one morning in the middle of the month, Nancy stared down at her water bucket, her heart pounding. A firm crust of ice lay over the water. They could no longer pretend that winter was still far off.

All around, as Nancy walked or balanced herself on Lightning while he carefully picked his way step by step over the rugged terrain, Nancy noticed the rush. Squirrels hurried and trembled over their nuts. Birds called in frantic tones. On some of the trees the leaves were already turning yellow. There was no game. Beavers, possum, deer, mountain sheep—all kept themselves hidden, and there was no time to stop and track them down.

"Only one thing left to do," said Hinshaw one day in his thin, wheezing voice. "We've been bringing our food up with us all along."

Bidwell nodded. "We'll share by turns. Hinshaw and I will be first."

So they killed the first ox.

By some uncanny sense, the animal seemed to know what was coming. As Hinshaw, Bidwell, and Brolaski approached, it began to groan. For a moment it stared fixedly at the men, then turned its head seeking refuge, and finding no escape, laid back its head in a long, mournful lowing.

Nancy felt a sharp twisting inside her own breast as the creature gave its final bellow. All her life she had helped to butcher lambs, hogs, and chickens. But those were farm animals, destined for the table from the start. The ox was different. He'd been bought and trained as a worker, and work he did until the flesh was worn thin on his bones. Then, to be eaten . . .

The meat was tough and stringy. Still they kept the fire going all night to smoke what remained, and as it shrank in the process, there was little left to save.

They drew lots for the next ox. It fell to Ben and Nancy. They killed their Bright and shared the meat, Nancy claiming the tail as an extra portion, for soup.

Buck could easily pull the wagon alone now, but he kept looking for his partner. It was sad to see.

More and more, the wagon was to Nancy like a home, a place to sleep, to change her clothes, or just to get away from the men for a spell. But the wagon was falling apart. The axle was cracked nearly in half. Two spokes broke on the left rear wheel. Then came another steep descent, nearly ending in disaster.

Four men stood on the bank, having dug a foothold between the jutting rocks. Six men at the top held the ropes that were wound around a tree trunk, and slowly, slowly, they began to ease the wagon down. They strained and groaned, leaning away from the weight, and those below balanced and braced the descending bulk.

A cry rent the air and with it a cracking sound. Then the wagon hung by only one rope, the other having split, and the counterforce sent the wagon swinging like a dead body on the end of a noose.

For a moment it seemed the entire thing would be ended—wagon and men would lose their slight hold and all come down, crashing down in an avalanche of bones and splinters.

But somehow they brought the wagon safely down. They dragged themselves on to a small, green valley with good pasture and good, clean water. When they had made their camp and drawn water for supper, Ben spoke out.

"I'm going to ditch my wagon," he said. "There's no way we can keep this up and make California before the snow."

"You and your missus and baby will sleep on the ground?" Joseph Chiles stood rigid, amazed.

"We'll keep the tent," Ben replied.

Nancy only stared at him and felt her color rising.

"We'll pack our supplies on the ox," Ben added.

"If you want to borrow a mule," Bartleson said with a smile, "you can pay me when we get to California."

Ben shook his head slowly. "I've got no cash, nor hope of getting any very soon."

"Well, I don't aim to go broke on this trip," said Bartleson, "just because others didn't think to provide."

Talbot Green had been pacing, sucking loudly at his gold tooth. "I aim to keep my wagon," he said. "And I advise everyone else to do the same. Certainly, a lady needs at least that much protection and privacy."

Disconcerted, Nancy looked down at the ground.

Hinshaw shook his head as in a spasm. "It's impossible to pull wagons over these mountains!" he cried in a high voice.

"Maybe it's impossible for you, old man," Green replied rudely, "but not for me. Indians respect a wagon train. It's more civilized."

Ben shrugged. "I'm not telling anyone else what to do. I just know I can go faster without this wagon to worry about."

"Well, I've got to tote some goods," Green grumbled, "and I can't carry them on my back."

"I wish you luck, friend," said Ben. "Andy's scouted ahead, and he says the going's very rough. But if you can make it with your wagon, I congratulate you."

Later, when she and Ben were alone, Nancy asked him, trying hard not to sound angry, "How come you never discuss anything with me, Ben?"

He looked at her in surprise. "Well, Nancy, I've got to make those decisions. What good would it do to worry you about it?"

Silently she picked a tiny thorn from the side of her thumb. Her nails were all broken to the quick; her hands were cracked and cut. She could not get them clean anymore.

"I don't know. Might do good to talk about things."

"Talkin' never put meat on the table," he said brusquely.

She sighed, feeling dull and silent inside. At dusk he had caught a rabbit. They'd stewed it and feasted on it. Yes, he did know how to put meat on the table. He knew how to break a trail, too. Bartleson did all the yelling and fussing, but it was Ben who picked out the trail more and more these last weeks. Ben knew things that counted, would always know them. She ought to be glad.

"Ben," she said, "I want to learn to shoot."

"Now, Nancy . . ."

"I want to learn to hunt for myself, rabbits and such."

"Now, Nancy, come on." He sounded just like Sam, and Nancy began to feel a puffing-up inside her, the kind of exploding puffiness she had so often seen in Sadie's face.

Nancy took a deep breath, lowered her voice, and said calmly, "Ben Kelsey, I'm askin' you please to teach me how to shoot. I aim to learn. If you won't help me, I'll . . . I'll ask Mr. Dawson."

Ben stared at her. He opened his mouth. He clenched his fist, and his hand went to his side, and for a moment Nancy had visions of him raising his hand to hit her, as she had once seen a neighbor man do to his wife in Missouri. Still, she held firm, her mouth set in a line, her eyes blazing right at him.

Ben did not move for several moments. Then he stood up, yanked her by the arm, and said, "Come on, then. I don't plan to waste a whole lot of powder, so if you don't learn fast, Nancy, you might as well forget it. Now, squat down on your knee, like that, and brace the rifle against your shoulder. Like this. No! You're pointing it too far to the side! No! There. That's it. Now, you pull back. It's gonna kick. I don't think you'll like it, Nancy."

"When do I pull? When?"

"Just easy," he said. "Keep your sight on the target. Get that tree. See the lightning burn in that tree? Aim for it. Squeeze back easy."

She aimed. She held. She kept the spot before her eye, thinking, thinking harder than she had ever thought of anything in her life, thinking she must, must, must hit it right and true, and as she thought, she squeezed the trigger and—shot.

A huge sigh came from Ben. He told her, "Hold the rifle down, now." He went to inspect the tree. Then he returned. "Well you're off target. But," he said, without expression, "you did not miss the tree. So try again."

Hooper came ambling by to see, then Brolaski and Belden, Dawson and Hinshaw.

They stood by, sober, not even exchanging glances. They chewed tobacco, stared, said nothing.

Presently Ben stood up, pulling Nancy's arm again, muttering, "That's all for tonight." To the men he said nothing, and neither did Nancy. She just walked on beside Ben, still holding the rifle.

She had not carried a rifle before. It made her feel different. Taller. Her steps were longer, more striding. She dreamed that night of being out alone in the woods, stalking a buck, carrying the rifle, unafraid.

The next morning Ben labored for hours, trying to pack the ox. Bartleson watched him for a few minutes, then he turned abruptly away. "We're not going to wait while you fool around with this animal."

Ben continued to work. "I never asked you to wait. We'll catch up."

Andy stayed to help. He had brought an extra mule, and he offered it to Ben.

"I'm obliged, Andy," Ben said. "Frankly, I haven't got any money a'tall. Didn't think we'd need cash anyhow."

"We'll get cash a-plenty in California," Andy said. "You know about that Dr. Marsh? I hear he got rich in California. No reason we can't do the same."

"How'd he do it?" Ben asked.

"Think he makes Indians work for him."

"Captures them?"

"Yup. Think so."

They said nothing more but strained over the packs. No

sooner had they tied everything onto the ox than the whole pack slid off. It burst open under the animal's hoof, and goods went tumbling down the hillside. Even Ben began to curse.

At first Nancy didn't mind the delay. It gave her time to mend her shoes. The soles were worn nearly through and she patched them with a flap of hide. Now she was finished and impatient.

"Those trappers we saw," she said, "had special pack saddles. They didn't just lay everything on top of those animals."

"Well, they had mules," Andy snapped. "Oxen are harder to pack."

"Still, you have to have something to tie the things to," Nancy insisted.

Ben gave Nancy a sidelong glance, scratched his beard, then rushed to their empty wagon. He hurried back for his ax and began to hack at the floorboards.

"What are you doing?" cried Andy. "You gone plumb crazy?"

"She's right." Ben gave the board another whack. "I'm going to make a frame and then mount it onto the ox with ropes. Trouble is now it falls off every step he takes 'cause that critter's all lumps and muscles."

Within an hour the frame was made. Onto it Ben and Andy loaded all the tools and bedding, the tent, extra clothes, the necessary dishes. Matches, medicines, utensils, and Nancy's pewter jug were carefully put into the large saddlebags and packed onto the mule.

"All set," Ben said, surveying his handiwork. "It's a darn good job, if I say so myself."

"It was Nancy's idea," Andy muttered crossly, so that Nancy had to laugh.

She sobered quickly at the sight of their wagon, ravaged and tipped over on its side. Ben had also tossed out all their empty barrels, a stool, several extra tools, clothes, and a whole box of dishes.

"Anything else we can spare?" he called out.

"Well, I guess I can get along with just one pan."

"Good."

"And we can leave the kettle," Nancy said, "and maybe the extra lantern."

No farther than a stone's throw away, only half concealed by a wispy cottonwood, suddenly there stood an Indian. His weathered old face glowed, not with paint or grease, but with some other radiance that made the three of them stop.

Andy spoke first, a whisper. "What the . . ." and he stepped out, reaching for his rifle.

"No!" Ben held him back. The Indian had begun to sway, bowing his head, raising his arms to the sky while he chanted a prayer.

They watched, awed. Even without knowing a bit of his language, they knew the feelings of that Indian—joy, unutterable joy and gratitude to the Spirit that had led him here, had guided him to where riches lay, a reward for his faith, a good omen for his future.

"He's not armed," Ben whispered. "He came for our things."

"How did he know?" Nancy whispered.

Ben only shook his head. They had never seen an Indian like this before, his face aglow, praying. It made Nancy think back to the squaws at Fort Laramie. She'd seen one of them rocking her baby; she'd seen her lean over and kiss its forehead. She thought of this as they moved on now, the Indian following at a distance.

By late afternoon they found the others camped around a beautiful little freshwater lake. The Indian moved in behind them, and Ben explained his presence.

"Well, then there will be plenty more for him to be thankful for," said Bidwell. "We've decided to leave our wagons, too. That last cliff convinced us. Hooper says there's worse up ahead."

Talbot Green nodded to Ben. "I'll be the first to admit my

mistake," he said, "and thank you kindly if you'll show me how to pack this ox."

"This is powerful heavy," Ben said, shaking his head over Green's load. "Can't you leave some of it behind?"

"Never," said Green. "It's family goods. Heirlooms."

Nancy, watching them, wondered how long they might still have the oxen. Bidwell had begun, laughingly, to call them "our commissary." It was strange. On the trail you always had to trade off one evil against another. If you walked you wore out your shoes; if you rode you wore out your britches. As they ate the oxen, they lost their beasts of burden. How far could they walk with heavy packs on their backs? And after the oxen were eaten—what then? Mountain men sometimes survived on mule meat, and after the mules were all eaten, then . . . Nancy could not bear even to think of it. She stroked Lightning's mane, remembering how she used to brush it, so that the dark brown hair gleamed against the dappled brown-white of his neck.

Even the animals were afraid. In the darkness before dawn the oxen would wander into the tall grass and hide. It sometimes took hours to track them down. Then fights began.

"We're not going to wait for you!" Bartleson would yell, already mounted, frantic to start.

"You'll wait if you want to eat!" Bidwell shouted back, losing his temper at last.

"Why don't we just leave those damned oxen and get on!" shouted Grove Cook. "We can hunt for our food."

"Then do it!" shouted Bidwell. "There's nothing to hunt."

How the Indians survived was a mystery, and Nick Dawson puzzled over it endlessly, while Bartleson insisted that they were not like other men and did not need the same food.

Smiling again, Bartleson had a proposition. "Tell you what, boys," he said. "Tomorrow let's butcher another ox. Me and my men will smoke the meat and carry most of it. Next time we slaughter, another mess can have the biggest share."

It seemed a reasonable plan. One less ox to prod might make their progress faster. But the next day, after the meat was divided, Bartleson and his men stood packed and assembled.

"We're leaving," Bartleson shouted. "We're tired of all this jawin', sick of complaints. We don't aim to be stuck in these canyons come winter because of a passel of weak-kneed old men and greenhorns. Now, we're setting the pace. If you and those dumb oxen can keep up, fine. If not, you can all go to the devil."

15

Of Bartleson's eight riflemen, only Hooper remained behind. "The captain's wrong," he said brusquely, his jaw tight. "I'm staying with the rest of you."

The rest of them stood dumbfounded.

"If I ever catch up with that skunk," shouted someone, "I'll string him feet first to a tree."

"We can go back to Fort Hall," suggested another.

"Not a chance," said Chiles. "We're too far off."

Talbot Green, pale and grim, raised his hand for attention. "Vote to go back?" he asked. Nobody spoke. Then he nodded. "We'll continue."

It was already October, with the icy chill of night lasting long into the morning. As the cold came, they would need more food in their bellies, especially fat.

"We got three oxen left," said Hinshaw, taking stock, "six mules . . ."

"And eleven horses," said Dawson, looking away from Monte, who looked like an old street nag by now, filthy and thin.

"My flour's all gone," said Weber. "My barrels are all empty, in fact."

Nancy glanced at Cheyenne Dawson. He had developed a habit of reaching into his pockets again and again. Sometimes he kept a bone or two there from the last meal. Now he brought out his hand, empty, and Nancy saw that his cheeks were sunken and his eyes very large and round with hunger.

At first she refused to believe that Bartleson wasn't coming back. "He's probably just gone ahead to scout. You know how impatient he gets," she told Ben. "He'll be back by tomorrow, sure."

Ben kept silent, picking out a trail that skirted a steep canyon. Bartleson, unencumbered by oxen, had been able to cross straight over.

"He'll come back for more meat," Nancy persisted. "He wouldn't just leave us. Why, the folks back home might hear of it, and he's a proud man. . . ."

"Shut up, Nancy!" Ben shouted. "You're gettin' like Jessica! I never could stand a talkative woman."

It came like a blow, and she shrank back. Well, she'd show him. She wouldn't talk at all. Let him walk alone, then, without anybody for company.

But she saw how his back was bent, and she felt the weight of his burden. Everyone was counting on him. When Bartleson left, Bidwell had spoken for the others, saying, "I suppose it's up to you, Ben. You've proved yourself to be the best pathfinder among us."

Now Nancy moved on close behind Ben, listening for the sound of gunfire that would mean game for supper. She led Lightning most of the time now. His hooves were cracked and the feet inflamed from the jagged rocks and thorns. He had lost two of his shoes, and there was no metal to replace them, nor time to fashion them.

Sometimes, when the pain became too great, Lightning would halt, lifting his foreleg and bobbing his head to make Nancy notice.

"Keep that horse moving!" Ben would shout almost savagely.

"He'll move in a minute." Nancy knew he was shouting from fear. Every minute was vital. If the snow came, they would freeze here in these mountains, and no mistake. Without wagons, without proper tools to build shelters, without food, they would die in two days, maybe three.

Sometimes Nick Dawson would get a gleaming, dreamy look in his eyes. "Now, just keep a lookout for the big river," he would say over and over. "That big, wide river, flowing between the mountains. We can even make canoes and float into California! They said there's a river . . ."

Nancy watched him, anxious and afraid. His shirt was in tatters, and his face was scratched in a dozen places from sharp twigs and brambles. But it was the look in his eyes that sometimes frightened her, and the ravenous way he ate when there was food.

That night Hooper caught a deer. They consumed it nearly raw, and Nancy saw Nick put a bone in his pocket, and for the next two days he gnawed at it while he rode. It was he who first spotted the river, and he wept. But three days later, when it became clear that this river would not surge and swell and send them smoothly floating into California—it ended with a trickle and a patch of mud in a dry river bed—Dawson was stupefied. He shook his head over and over, staring at the huge, horrible mountains that still loomed ahead. "My God, look at those mountains up ahead!" His face was pasty white. "There is no river," he said. "No river. I'll lie down here and die."

"Now, look up, 'Cheyenne.'" Ben and Bidwell took him up by the arms. "See those Injun fires? Let's us go see and maybe trade our butcher knives for some food."

They returned several hours later, having swapped and smoked the pipe, with one large roasted fish and a basketful of nuts. Divided up, it made three bites of fish and a handful of pine nuts for each.

"Don't know whether to eat them all at once," Nick said, smiling slightly, "or stretch them out one at a time."

Nancy ground up several nuts for Ann, then gave her the last of the pemmican, dried meat pounded into a paste, mixed with animal fat. It tasted horrible, but Ann sucked greedily at the little skin bag containing the gluey mass. Fitzpatrick had given it to her. "It's what the Injuns use to keep going," he'd said. Now it too was gone. Gone, like their wagon, like their clothes and tools and dishes—sacrificed. One by one she'd had to leave everything behind, everything she needed or cared about. Except for Ben and Ann.

She looked down at Ann, and suddenly a terrible feeling seized her. Oh, Lord! What if Ann were to die?

In the night she awakened, her stomach twisted in hunger, thinking it over and over—what if Ann were to die? Then came the dreams. Nearly every night she dreamed of Pa. Pa bringing in a buck. Pa in the guise of Bartleson, calling her a weakling. She dreamed of Lightning, but he was only the size of a dog, and then there were only bones in a pile, half-hidden in prairie grass, until she picked one up and it turned into a rifle.

Dreams became banquets of all the food she had eaten in her entire life. When she woke up, her mouth watered, and then came the bitter taste of bile lasting all day long.

Nancy envied Nick his bones. She began to gnaw on a peeled stick.

Nick Dawson had taken to circling out while they proceeded, searching for baskets of seed hidden by Indians, stalking wherever some of them were camped, to learn their ways of finding food.

One day he ran toward the others, breathless, his hands filled with a strange, sticky stuff, and he shouted out, "Food! Honeydew. Indians eat it—they find it in the tule grass. It's sweet as honey!"

He held out some to Nancy, and she took it, feeling the texture with her fingertips, inhaling the sweetness, nearly fainting from desire.

"Is there more?" she asked, half afraid to begin.

"Plenty. The rushes are loaded with it. The Indians just go pick it off," Nick said, licking his lips.

"Mmm." Nancy ran her tongue over the sweet mass, and immediately she consumed the whole handful and was ravenous for more.

"Ben!" He was beside her in an instant. Together they rushed to the tule swamp where they stood ankle-deep in water, gathering the food. The others came, Hinshaw laughing with delight, Bidwell speaking of manna from heaven, all of them stuffing the sweet food into their mouths.

Coarse as bran, sweet as syrup, it was indeed like heaven-sent fare, satisfying their need to chew, filling them quickly.

It was after she had given Ann her fill, and the baby lay quiet for the first time in weeks, that Nancy noticed the small, black speck. It was on the baby's chin. It moved slightly, caught in the sticky substance. Then she saw tiny, tiny feelers, and she gasped. "Ben." It was a quaking whisper. "Ben—look. Do you know what we're eating?"

Ben, too, stared down closely at the greenish-brown balls of stuff clinging to the rushes. He stared up at Nancy. "My God," he whispered. "It's—just—bugs. Bugs stuck together in—in the sap. That's what made it so—so *crisp*."

Again the dreams, the waking in the night, Ma's face before her so clear, so plain. Oh, the dear face! Was it an omen? Could something be wrong? Might she never, never see Ma again at all?

Nancy looked up into the sky, as if to search for some sign. Not even a star was visible through the moist, clinging haze of night. She tried to pray, but only emptiness followed, and her body began to ache.

"You all right?" Ben mumbled. Soon someone would wake him to stand watch. With so few of them, it was a rare night that a man could sleep clear through.

"I'm all right," she whispered, but she felt a twinge in her stomach. It was the familiar ache, first the dull nagging at the small of her back, then from deep within, like a small bubble breaking, that twisting feeling, more pressure than pain, the feeling that said, remember, you are a woman. Each month it reminded her, and each month since it had started, when she was thirteen, she had marveled that this strange breaking inside had something to do with having children.

Now she turned on her side, moaning slightly.

"You sick?"

"The—the usual monthly."

"Oh."

She was always embarrassed by it. She had been thankful that since Ann's birth it had not happened. But now . . . oh, Lord. She folded her hands again. "Oh, Lord, please let me wait until we get to California! Please, Lord, I feel so sick when I'm with child!"

She breathed deeply. That always helped. It also made her think more clearly. Thank goodness she'd saved plenty of rags. She'd try to ride tomorrow instead of walking. That would help. As for babies—since they'd left the others at Soda Springs, there had been no time for her and Ben, and no privacy, except once. Just once, the night before they abandoned the wagon, they had lain in it together, so close, so safe under the canvas top, soft on Ma's lovely quilt . . .

She breathed out in a sigh. By morning she'd be feeling fine. . . . But in the morning she was doubled up, knees drawn to her chest, with pains nearly as bad as she'd had in giving birth to Ann.

She sat up, then tried to stand, but reason left her and the next thing she remembered the ground had risen up at a crazy tilt and smacked her, hard, on the side of the head.

Hands lifted her. It was just barely dawn. Nancy could see a strip of crimson lying across the sky, and the dark-blue mist above. For a moment she did not know whether it was sunrise or sunset.

"Anybody got provisions left?" Someone called it along the line. Nancy heard the grumbling answers. "No. No, all's gone. Been gone for weeks, don't you know?"

Someone produced a few pine nuts, sticky and dirty.

"Here, Nancy. You eat these."

"I can't. I don't want . . ."

"Take them, ma'am," said Nick Dawson, looking down at

her. His posture and his expression made her feel that she was dead and all the men had come to stand around muttering prayers, regrets. If she died, she wondered, would they really care? Would these men stop long enough for her to be buried?

Weakling! Baby! Stupid! She forced herself to sit up and, grasping Ben's arm, pulled herself to her feet. "I suppose I'll ride today," she said, smiling weakly. "Ben, just bring Lightning. Maybe you'll hold Ann for a while. Just for a while."

For several hours she held to the reins with both hands. Then, somehow, they had slipped from her hands, and she had slumped forward, her head dropping down onto the horse's neck.

When she opened her eyes again the sun blinded her. The dry, acrid smell of stinkweed engulfed her, made her throat sting.

"I'm going to leave you here for a while, Nancy," Ben was saying.

"Where are the others?" The sun beamed straight into her eyes, so that she had to shield them with her hands.

"I—they got ahead of us," Ben said brusquely.

"Everyone?"

"Just a little ways ahead, I expect," Ben said. He was smiling, and Nancy knew by the manner of his smile that he, too, was fighting panic.

"Now, don't be scared, Nancy," he said. "I just slowed down 'cause I knew you were doing poorly. Thought to ease up and let you rest. Before I knew it, they got out of sight."

He cleared his throat, and again he brought that strange smile which was too brittle, too bright. "I'll catch up with them and tell them to wait up for us; then I'll come back for you. So you just stay here with Lightning. . . ."

"Ben! Ben! What if you don't find them? What if you get lost? I'd better come with you."

He stood before her, holding Lightning's head, unsmiling now and firm. "Nancy, it's best you stay here. It would slow me down to have to take you. Then we'd be in real trouble. Alone, I can cover twice the ground. Nancy!" He took her hand for a moment, then said briskly, "Look, you'll be just fine. Here, you take Ann on your lap. Get down off the horse, Nancy."

She stared at him, unflinching. "No," she said.

"What? Nancy, get down. You can just sit here by these trees and rest. . . ."

"No."

He shrugged. "All right, then. Stay on the horse if you want. But don't you leave here!" Then his voice became soft. "I'll be back soon as I can. Before dark. Don't you worry."

He thrust out the rifle. "Here," he said. "You keep this with you."

"Ben!" Visions darted past her mind. What manner of beasts might come to attack her here alone on this mountain? "Ben, why would I need a gun?"

"In case you see a rabbit running by," he said, and in another moment he had disappeared into the brush, and she was alone.

16

She had been alone before. In the Missouri woods where she lived as a little child with no neighbors for miles, the wind used to screech through the chinks, and every day it took forever for the sun to move across the sky. There was nobody to talk to. Nobody but Ma, and she was busy tending babies—always babies to feed, to wash, to bury. Pa was out hunting or digging or fence-mending, always too set on his work to pay her any mind, unless to send her running back to the house for something or to correct her. "Nancy, that's downright foolishness! You should be ashamed."

She had been lonely, yes, but never entirely alone.

Now she sat on Lightning and felt as if the earth were buckling beneath her. She clutched Ann, hearing every turn of a leaf. The rifle lay across her saddle. She would keep her eyes tightly closed.

If she opened them, surely she would find herself back home again, wouldn't she? Home in Pa's cabin, with Ma at the washtub, rabbit stew bubbling in the kettle, a baby crying from the cradle, and maybe Pa come pounding in, setting his rifle down by the door, asking, "Nancy been good?"

"Very good." Ma smiled. "Helped me with the wash today."

She would keep her eyes closed and then find that all this was just a dream and her real self still back there. She'd run to Pa and feel the roughness of his beard against her cheek.

He was not a kissing man, but when she came to him, he would kneel down, and for a moment she would rub her soft, warm cheek against his bristly, cold one.

She had loved him, but never said the word. In church, the few times they all went together—when they lived near enough and all had shoes to wear and none were sick—she sat beside Pa, and while the preacher spoke of God, she visualized him exactly. God had a brown beard and a wide chest, strong arms, and eyes so blue and keen they could see everything. They could even see what a little girl was thinking.

She would just keep her eyes closed and stay here forever. If Ben was lost or killed, if he never returned, she would still be sitting here with her eyes tightly closed, even when the snow started to fall, swirling all around, burying her, and when at last she opened her eyes, she would be back there, six years old again, in Missouri.

Nancy had never been so terrified. It was the wind, she thought dimly, the wind in the pines that was moaning so, like a man sick to dying.

Something was wrong with her. Born scared, probably. Pa used to talk about folks like that, and he'd spit with disgust. She was the only one that was like that, born scared.

Once Ma had been getting wood out back of the cabin when three naked Indians snuck up behind her. Nancy had run to hide, but Ma, calm as anything, picked up a split log, waved it overhead, and cried out, "You savages get away from me or I'll kill you!"

They had understood by her stance and her tone that she was not afraid, so they turned tail and ran. But Nancy, too scared even to peek out from behind the wood pile, had kept her eyes tightly shut, trembling in every limb. Born scared.

And Grandma, even when she was old, fifty at least, had gone to a neighbor's to help tend a sick mother and child. She came across a grizzly bear big as life, black and mean, claw raised up and teeth showing. Grandma just stood there stock still and outstared that grizzly, not closing her eyes, not running away, but holding her ground.

But she, Nancy, was born scared. Scared of river crossings, snakes, Injuns—scared of today . . .

There at her feet comes a rattlesnake ready to strike, mean and deadly. It leaps up onto Lightning's back, attacks Nancy, bites her leg, her thigh, reaches out its ugly head to Ann's little hand, but Nancy jumps out of the saddle, drags the snake down behind her, beats it again and again with her rifle butt until it lies dead, flat, mangled, and then she cuts open her own leg to suck out the poison. . . .

Right then three Indians come sneaking up, the evil intention clear in their eyes, one leering, another reaching for Lightning's halter, the third holding a spear. Nancy sits straight. She thrusts out her rifle, throws back her head, shouts out in a tone of stern authority, "Get out! This is my place. If you so much as touch my horse, I will kill you all. I shoot fast and true. The last Injun who dared to insult me had his head blown clean off. Back! Back! And keep your eyes from my child!" They back away meekly, astounded at the strength of a woman. . . .

And from his winter lair, plodding on heavy feet, aching with hunger comes the brown bear, sees her, claw uplifted, looks around, waiting to encircle her, to knock her down and trample her, mangle the child; but she is swift and certain. She lets go the shot at the very instant the bear begins his forward leap, shoots him straight in the heart, then again between the eyes. The bear staggers, halts, falls. When Ben comes he says, "What's that?" She says, "A bear. I killed him for supper." And he says, "Nancy, I'm surprised. I sure do admire your skill with a gun. Thought you'd be scared up here all alone." And she says, "No. Not at all. I was busy killin' this here bear and catching a snake and chasing away three Injuns. See, I can take care of myself and Ann just fine." And he says, "That's so, Nancy. You are braver than your ma or grandma." And he takes off his hat.

A slight rattling noise made her jump. Her eyes flew open. She snatched up the rifle. Nothing. Whatever it was, she saw no danger. Probably just a dry pine cone rattling to the ground.

Now Nancy gazed down at the ground with its scattering of pine cones of all sizes and shapes. She moved her eyes around and focused on the pine needles. They made a soft brown bed under the tree. She gazed up ahead. Small, delicate saplings had sprouted among the tall, thick timbers of pine, birch, and oak. She followed the trunk of a great pine tree up and up, so that the sun's rays slanted down between the boughs, and she saw the fine, hazy bits of dust that made a beam of sunlight, and she reckoned she might sit here all day just looking at that beam of sun, thinking about it, figuring out what caused it to stay like that, all together in a piece, what made it glow so brightly, and seeing how it touched the pine needles turning the tips into silver.

Why had she never really seen a pine tree and a sunbeam before? Her throat suddenly felt tight. There was still much to see. She did not want to die.

For a long time she watched the sun slanting through the pine boughs. Then she noticed a small brown bird pecking at the bark. She marveled at the perfect, tiny claw-feet clinging to the bark while it pecked so very hard. Bees and flies and moths appeared—had they been there all along? They made a clear, humming chorus, so that the wind's moan seemed softer. A squirrel darted out from a bed of dry leaves, rolling a nut in front of itself. Another squirrel came, pouncing down to steal the nut, and the first squirrel reared up, then chased the thief away, and Nancy laughed aloud. It made Ann laugh, too, and she made little cooing sounds, "Gee! Da!" as if she were trying, in her delight, to talk. The baby's voice filled Nancy, filled her completely with happiness.

How much there was to see and feel! She pulled the shawl back from her shoulders to feel the sun's warmth. She half closed her eyes, so that the light came filtering between her dark lashes, soft and warm. She undid the braid and let her hair blow loose to catch the feel of the wind. Dimly she heard a scolding voice from her past, "Hair hanging down like a hussy!" She shook her head to make her hair crackle, and she breathed deeply, taking in the pine, thistle, wild grass, rock, and soil.

How had a day ever passed without her noticing the many things of the world? Nancy was aghast. Why, she could spend a lifetime just noticing and never be done. She'd never noticed that tiny white flowers, no bigger than tomato seeds, blossomed on the very tips of slender green grasses. Now, as she gazed, she realized that every plant did flower. Everything flowered and seeded and budded, over and over again. The same purple wildflowers that grew back home grew on the prairie, and they also grew here in little shelves of rock. They survived wherever they happened to land.

Nancy slipped down from her horse. She took off her cloak and set Ann down on the ground beside her. Ann could sit up fine now, without Nancy's knee to prop her up. Nancy picked bits of wild grass and clover and vines, and she studied them, holding them out for the baby to see, too. Each pebble on the ground was different from every other, veined with silver, white, or brown. The pebbles themselves had a dozen different colors.

Without fear, the thought came upon her: maybe this would be her very last day. Well, if she was going to die, at least this would be a day full of wonders.

Holding Ann, letting Lightning follow, Nancy set out to see the world.

When Ben came, it was already near sunset. His face was drawn, his expression anxious.

"Nancy! Nancy, are you all right?" He broke through the thickets.

"I'm fine." Her voice was low, but strong.

"You eat anything?"

"I found some wild rhubarb and blackberries," Nancy said.

"Where?"

"Oh, a piece further on. Near a stream."

"You went to a stream, away from here?"

"Just a mile or so, I reckon." She pointed. "Over yonder, down that hill. I heard it from here."

He looked at her strangely, head cocked. "You all right?"

"I sat by the stream. Had Ann with me, and she played with the wet pebbles. Ben, they're all colors when you really look at them. Especially when they're wet."

"You all right, Nancy?"

"I saw a beaver swimming by in the middle of the stream." She had thought momentarily of shooting it, then searching for the body, to eat the meat.

"I didn't want to shoot it," she said.

"It would have sunk anyhow," Ben said. "You couldn't have gotten it."

"I didn't *want* to shoot it," she tried to explain. "It was alone. Like me." She fumbled for words. "I mean . . ."

Ben only nodded. "We'd best get moving. Maybe catch up to the rest of 'em by midnight." He was already looking past her, worry and exhaustion plain on his face. He didn't really understand. He didn't know how it felt to be one with the tree, the rocks, the wind, the beaver. Perhaps some day she would know how to tell him.

Ten days after he had abandoned them, Bartleson and his men came staggering into camp at noon, more dead than alive. Four days earlier they had eaten some rotten fish and spent the succeeding days and nights in agony. Bartleson, sickest of all, was gaunt-faced, and even his once thick arms were shrunken to half their girth.

To draw breath evidently pained him, but he managed a faint smile and a wave. "If I ever get back to Missouri, boys," he gasped, "I'll gladly eat out of the trough with my hogs."

They forgave him.

17

★★

One night in the middle of October it snowed. Even before she opened her eyes Nancy knew it by the sharpness in the air and the numb silence. In the past, the season's first snow had always been a happy time. Now it meant catastrophe.

In an hour or so the snow had melted, but it left a warning so stern that all day they verged on panic, solemn, silent, their faces haggard.

By afternoon they had ascended a high rock mountain. They stopped short as the cliffs abruptly ended, pitching down into a canyon so steep that all seemed lost. With gigantic trees and boulders to match, it appeared to have been set by the hands of giants, so that they were mere specks of life, too insignificant to matter.

"I think we can get through," said Jimmy-John, gazing across the canyon. His horse, undaunted, strained and pawed at the ground, ready to leap down the forbidding precipice.

"That horse of yours could probably climb a tree," said Bidwell, but without smiling. "What about the rest of us?"

"I'm willing to go ahead and see," said Jimmy-John, holding back his horse with effort.

"Why don't both of you go," suggested Ben. "The rest of us will wait up here. If it looks good, fire a shot and we'll follow."

It was an uneasy resting place, high on the promontory, and nobody unpacked the animals. Often the animals slept with their packs on, just as men slept without even spreading their blankets, too exhausted to do more than lay their heads down on their saddles.

Andy, having set his horse to graze, joined Ben and Nancy. "I should have gone with them." Sullenly he picked at a hole in his boot. "Jimmy-John's too crazy. He'd jump off a cliff with that horse of his and expect the rest of us to do the same."

"Bidwell's with him," Ben said, picking up Ann and bouncing her on his knee. "He's sensible enough."

"Da!" Ann squealed, reaching for Ben's beard. "Da-da!"

Ben looked down at the baby, his lips softening to an expression Nancy had seen only a few times before. The sorrowful tenderness in Ben's eyes brought a catch to her throat.

"She's saying 'daddy,'" Nancy whispered.

He nodded and clapped Ann's little hands together, singing softly, "I gave my love a cherry without a stone . . ."

Suddenly he stopped and almost fiercely he demanded, "What happened to *your shoes?*"

"They're all torn up, Ben."

"Nancy, you can't . . ."

"I've saved the pieces of leather," she said, bringing them from her pocket. "When we get to California . . ." but the words stuck in her throat.

Two shots rang out, reverberating like a cannon, and Bartleson, already astride his horse and in a heat to leave, gave the signal. Hounded by the snow of the night, a frantic haste seized them all. Panic was transmitted to the beasts; the mules began to kick and gallop, the oxen ran wild-eyed and frantic, hurtling their huge bodies into shrubs and trees. The horses ran, nearly unmanageable, whinnying and snorting as if they sensed sweet pasture and clear water, though all that lay on the canyon slopes were jagged rocks and thistles and ruts.

Suddenly Bidwell came scrambling up, motioning and shouting, "Go back!"

"What the hell are you yelling about!" Bartleson barely stopped to listen, shaking his fist, spurring his horse.

"You can't get through," shouted Bidwell, waving his arm. "It's too narrow!"

"But the shot. We heard a shot. . . ."

"Jimmy-John shot off his dragoon pistol—the idiot. Not even a bird could get through that place. . . ."

"Then where's Jimmy-John?"

"Well, maybe *he* can get through. Listen, go back."

But the momentum had already carried them past the point of turning, and in their wildness men fired off pistols to make the animals run, until in total exhaustion they stopped at last and stood in darkness on the canyon slopes, unable to continue, yet too spent to go back.

"We'll have to leave them," Brolaski said finally.

"On this cliff?" Dawson shook his head. "They'll die."

"We'll have to go back up and camp there," Ben said wearily. "But there's no water."

"There's water down at the bottom," Nancy said, and she felt a ripple of surprise among the men. "Mr. Bidwell told me," she continued. "We can go down and bring up water for the animals."

"We haven't enough buckets." Someone laughed rudely.

"Well, you can bring it in your boots then," retorted Ben.

"She's right," Josiah Belden added. "Without water those animals won't last the night."

They picked grass from the canyon slopes. Ben stuffed it into the front of his jacket, and grimly he said, "Now I'll go feed your darling."

"Ben!" She reached out, wanting to talk to him. There was no longer any time for talk between them, it seemed. He was always too weary, too burdened. She watched him go by the steady swing of his lantern, and she saw the white patches of Lightning's neck in the moonlight, hearing the echo of Ben's reproach, *your darling.*

Twice Ben went down with grass. Returning, he sank down on his knees. "I'll go back for water."

"No," she said. "I'll go. You rest now."

"Nancy! You can't. Those cliffs are slippery."

"You just watch Ann," she said. "I can get water."

"That dumb ox won't take it!" he warned.

"I'll make him take it," she muttered. "Mr. Dawson!" she called as Nick hurried past with his bucket. "Can we go together? I'll hold your lantern. . . ."

They made their way down the slope, slick as ice in spots, and Nick sat down and slid by the seat of his britches. Nancy hesitated for a moment, then followed.

"I—I never saw a lady do that," Dawson said, grinning.

"I guess you never saw a lady pour water down an ox's throat, either," she replied, "but that's what I'm going to do."

They pressed their way between thorny thickets to the stream, dipped in their buckets, and at last Nancy found Buck collapsed on the hillside, barely breathing.

"There, now," she murmured. She dipped her hand into the water and rubbed it onto his muzzle, his throat. "Drink it, Buck," she murmured. She reached into the huge mouth, felt the slime of the great teeth, the thick tongue, working her fingers back until at last the ox threw back its head and its mouth hung wide open, and she cried, "Pour!" and Dawson obliged.

Twice more they watered the ox, then Nancy brought a full bucket for Lightning. By the time she returned to lie down beside Ben, she was shaking with cold and fatigue. As her feet thawed, the pain came in great searing waves. She slept at last, dreaming that she walked on fire, that Ben came with water in his boots, the drops seeping out as he went, so that by the time he reached her none was left.

Six days later they killed the last ox. They pressed on, deep into the mountains. Now and again a rifle shot would ring out, and a man would retrieve a crow or a hawk. They ate anything that flew or crawled or burrowed. They ate grubs and worms and grasshoppers fried to a crisp. Sometimes they were lucky enough to find acorns. They cracked them and pounded them into mush and leached them until the water ran clear, but still the bitter taste remained; they hated acorns more than anything—that bitter Indian food.

Bartleson, half-crazed with hunger, took off again with a string of three horses. He returned, chastened and weeping. In the night the Indians had stolen two of his horses. Horse meat was the redskin's main food in these mountains; he had come upon their camp and seen bones, nothing but bones in ghastly heaps—the bones of horses captured and consumed.

Talbot Green, too, had lost his horse. "We'll take turns on Monte," Nick Dawson said, clapping him on the back.

Green nodded, still toting his heavy load wrapped in canvas. His fine shirt was in rags, covered over with a blanket of buffalo, poorly cured and scraped. It hung like bark on his shoulders, stiff and soiled. His hair had grown frizzled and wild; even the fancy gold tooth could no longer grace his features.

"I'm worried about Green," Dawson told Ben soberly. "He can't keep up. Yesterday he was a full three miles behind us."

Ben nodded. "He'll have to cache his things. It's just a matter of time before he concludes it."

But while the others gave in and buried their remaining possessions and marked the spot with rocks and twigs, Talbot Green only stood by, shaking his head.

They buried camp kettles and buckets and furs. Someone buried a whole cask of whiskey, another a toolbox. Nancy and Ben sorted through their poor possessions, spread them out on the ground, and wordlessly made two piles. They kept one pot, a tin cup for each of them, two blankets, an ax, a knife, a hammer, the clothes on their backs, and Ma's quilt.

Ben dug a hole two feet deep. Into it he laid Ann's cradle, then their tent, remaining household things, even the bucket. He stopped, his hands on the pewter jug. "Nancy, you sure you want to . . . you don't have to. . . ."

"Leave it!" she said, her teeth clenched. She looked around, and there stood Talbot Green, watching from a distance, still dragging his load. Boldly she met his eyes until he turned away, and some time later she saw him walking off with Grove Cook, the two of them whispering, planning.

He returned, finally, looking weak and beaten, and he wiped the back of his hand across his face like a boy just done crying. "I cached my stuff," he said. "I can't carry it anymore."

What he promised Grove Cook in return for standing watch over the spot that night, nobody knew. But in the stillness of night several shots rang out, and in the morning Grove Cook dragged in the stiff, dead body of an Indian.

"Caught him trying to steal Green's stuff," he said. "He won't steal no more."

Now when they rode out, Ma's quilt lay across Lightning's back, over the saddle, and Nancy tried to make a joke of it. "Imagine how we'll look, Ben! I expect we'll be the only folks ever to ride into Californ-y on such a fancy-covered horse."

Bidwell, just behind them, gave a harsh chuckle. "You'll be the only folks ever did ride into California anyhow," he said. "Nobody's done it. Not all the way. For sure, no women."

"You're the first, Nancy," Ben said, and again she saw the grieving expression of his mouth, the tenderness in his eyes that was more frightening than his anger.

"Ben, how will we know when we get to California?"

"Well, it's on the edge of the ocean. You can't miss it."

She only nodded, afraid of her thoughts. Maybe Ma was right and there really was no place called California, but somebody just invented it, and they would keep walking forever and forever, seeking a place that didn't exist. Maybe it was like heaven, a place people talked about but could never prove.

"I sometimes think," Dawson said, his voice dazed, "it might be kinder to Monte to kill him. I see his eyes . . ."

"No," Nancy said softly. "Monte will be all right. He's strong."

The path narrowed, winding around and down, until it

became a ledge just barely wide enough for one person to go. Above them huge rocks jutted out into the path. Ben, moving slowly behind Nancy, steadied her with his voice, "Easy, Nancy, easy." Ben was bringing Hinshaw, half-holding, half-dragging the old man, having tied a rope between them, with Bidwell behind Ben, bringing along the few remaining animals.

Nancy heard a cry, first the cry of a man, then the scream of a horse, and she stopped dead still as ahead of her Dawson lay flat, his legs over the edge, holding on to Monte whose pack had struck a rock, nearly sending him down.

"Hang on!" came the shouts from behind. "Dawson! Let 'im go if you have to!"

Silently Nancy prayed, clutching Ann, holding Lightning, feeling as if she stood alone at the very top of the world, all her senses straining to give the help she could not offer.

Somehow Dawson managed. Monte picked his way again over the faint trail worn by mountain goats or sheep. Nick turned and, seeing Nancy, smiled slightly, a smile of victory. His gaze held hers for a long moment. Then he looked down at her feet, and she saw him flush and bite his lip. She had not been aware that her feet were bleeding.

As they continued their descent, Nancy's side began to ache so sharply that she had to let Lightning follow on his own. Some of the animals, worn to the point of extremity, simply lay down and died. Others lost their footing on the treacherous cliffs and fell all the way down, so that even their packs could not be retrieved.

Some of the men, including Nick and Andy, began to rush down to the bottom of a ravine whenever a mule went over. Half a dozen men dragged it up by the feet. Then the body, still warm, was split in half, the heart torn out, warm and pulsing, and sometimes eaten on the spot, raw and dripping.

Like wolves smelling meat, the others came running. They cut away the flesh with their knives and barely braised it over hastily built fires before they ate.

"Eat!" Ben held out a hunk of pink flesh to Nancy. It had

been scraped from the flank of Bartleson's wagon mule, the Badger.

"I—it's too raw."

"Eat!"

She chewed and chewed, and at last she swallowed. There was no time to boil water for broth. There was no time to jerk and smoke meat. No time. Now they gave her the soft, warm intestines.

"Eat it, Mrs. Kelsey," Bidwell urged. "The Indians eat these raw, and they draw strength from them."

Nancy, staring at him, opened her mouth, took in the soft, stringy mass, and, without chewing, swallowed. She held her breath, counting to twenty, her eyes bulging, needing all her will to keep it down, making herself think of rabbit stew, bear steaks, onions and potatoes, mulberry wine, apple pie, *anything*.

Once someone caught a coyote. Even the tail was scraped clean and eaten. Josiah Belden, lying under a tree in the night, had the good luck to spot a wildcat and aim at the green glow of its eyes.

"Yipee-eii!" he screamed out, rising on the spot to build a fire and cook his wildcat, taking care to cook it properly, chattering and shouting all the while, then handing it around like a hero, giving the innards to old Hinshaw who sat with his hands out, weeping like a beggar.

"I haven't et in three days," the old man whimpered. "I haven't had any bread in three weeks. I can't live without bread." He gazed all around. "Johnny! You got any flour left? Any left in the box?"

He found Bidwell and went to him, arms outstretched. "You'll give me some bread, won't you? I teamed up with you, Johnny. I let you take my ox and my wagon. . . ."

"I gave you the last of the flour, don't you remember?" Bidwell's face was flushed, and he tried to hold off the old man.

"Ah, Johnny, it's no use." Hinshaw sighed, and he lay down

full-length beside the fire. He lay without moving. Nancy could see that he was neither sleeping nor fully awake, and by dawn he still had not moved a muscle.

"Catch up! Catch up!" Bartleson shouted, and others echoed the call and the morning move was on.

Still Hinshaw lay with his eyes wide-open, dazed.

"Come on, old man." Bidwell prodded him. "Get up. We're off to California!" He made his voice cheerful. "First one up," he teased, "gets a dozen flapjacks for breakfast!"

Nancy bent over the old man and laid her head on his chest. She rubbed his hands. "No fever," she said, "and he's breathing steady."

"What is it, then?"

"Nothing, except I'm tired, Johnny," came the high, thin voice. "I know when I'm done. Even a dumb animal knows when it's reached the end of his rope. This is my time, Johnny. I ain't moving."

"Hinshaw!" Bidwell grasped him by the arms, shouting, "Get up, for God's sake."

"I ain't moving, Johnny." Hinshaw's chin jutted out firmly. "No matter what you say, I aim to die here. These old bones of mine just can't push anymore. Even if you tried to carry me, I'd just fold up on you and die. Just don't make a fuss. I can't stand to hear a fuss. . . ."

Suddenly a rifle shot blasted through the air, and the bullet whipped directly over the old man's head, striking a tree above him to send the bark shattering down.

"Ben!" Nancy screamed. "For God's sake . . . Ben!"

He stood just a horse's length away, his rifle leveled, as fierce and determined as Nancy had ever seen him.

"You get up," Ben ordered harshly, eyes narrowed. "You get up this moment, old man, or I'll shoot you where you lie. I haven't pushed through these mountains and dragged your carcass across rivers and over cliffs for you to tell us you give up. Now, move!"

"You wouldn't," the old man whimpered. "Johnny wouldn't

let you, and neither would your wife. That sweet young woman wouldn't let you shoot me, lad."

Nancy sprang up. She stood beside Ben, her arms folded tightly across her chest to keep from shaking. "Shoot him, Ben," she said.

Ben laid the rifle to his shoulder. He bent his head to the sight.

"He's an old fool and a coward," Nancy said, her voice ringing out so loud that it echoed in her own ears. "I'm going to count to three, Ben, then you shoot." Her hands were clenched so hard that her nails dug into her palms. "One! Two!"

"Now, lad, wait . . . you wouldn't . . ."

A shot rang out, ricocheted back with a ping, and the old man leapt to his feet, cursing, hopping up and down in rage. "Move out!" Ben thundered, louder than ever Fitzpatrick had done. "Moo-oove out!" and as he gave the signal, the wide sweep of his hand, everyone obeyed.

That night when they lay on the ground, their blanket barely keeping out the dampness, Ben began to shiver uncontrollably.

"I really would have shot him, Nancy," he whispered. "I don't know what got into me."

"You made him get up," she said. In the darkness she smiled. "You were wonderful." She touched his face, and her hand came away wet and clammy. "Ben! You're feverish!"

"I would have shot him, Nancy. I really would have *shot him!*"

He mumbled it again and again, between shivering and shaking.

"Ben! You're freezing! Move close to me." She would warm him with her own body, take away the chills, the fever. She pulled the quilt tightly over him.

He slept fitfully for half an hour or so. Then he sat bolt upright, sweat streaming from his face, and he began violently to vomit.

"Ben! Ben!" He retched, dry heaves, for he'd eaten nothing all day, then he doubled over, his body wracked and writhing, until the very trembling made him sleep again.

He awakened, his eyes rolling and desperate. "Don't tell them! Have Andy put me on the horse. Tie me on. . . ." Then he was silent, unconscious.

18

All night Nancy sat with her arms around Ben, rocking to and fro. Nothing mattered anymore. It didn't matter where they had come from, where they were going. Ann cried out. It didn't matter. Lightning snorted, nuzzling her shoulder. It didn't matter. And when the sun came up, pink and gold and behind it the beautiful cool blue light, it didn't matter either. Without Ben nothing mattered. She felt now as if all other feelings had been only imitations of feelings. Never before had she known such pain—and such love.

The two feelings blended and twisted inside her, the one growing into the other, pain spreading and filling every limb, love reaching out to overwhelm even the pain, until she could not move from the weight of it.

Nick Dawson came around first. He gazed down at Ben. Tentatively he said, "Mrs. Kelsey? Nancy?"

She did not answer. She only sat holding Ben more tightly, unable to move, for the sharpness of love and pain held her rooted.

Dawson sent for the others. Josiah Belden reached into his pocket. "I've got some tablets..."

"He can't swallow anything," Nancy whispered. "He's unconscious."

"Is he breathing?" Bidwell bent down, touching Ben's pulse. "Just barely," he said, turning to the others who now all stood by, shuffling their feet, working their lips tonelessly, none daring to say it straight out, all thinking it, until Bartleson declared, "He can't travel."

"Sure not," said someone else. "He's too sick."

"We could make a litter for him," said Chiles. "We could carry him."

"If we were on flat ground, we could. Yeah, then we could."

"But it's canyons and cliffs, and he can't sit on a horse."

"Even if we tied him on . . ."

Nancy saw them all only as a shadow, a haze. She saw Andy standing off to one side, gazing away, saying nothing.

"He's too far gone. We'll have to leave him."

"Leave him here."

"We've got to keep moving. Snow in the air . . . he'll die anyhow."

Nancy felt a hand on her shoulder. In the sudden red-hot violence of rage she did not know whose hand it was, nor did she care. She leapt to her feet and grasped Ben's rifle and, bent like a wildcat ready to spring, she stood over Ben, facing them all. Something went off inside her, stronger and harder than any rifle exploding.

"You! You all keep away from me and my husband, do you hear? He's going to live! You say to leave him? I'll never leave him, never in a million years, never, if I lie here and freeze to death beside him. And I swear to God, the first man of you that gets on his horse or walks out to leave Ben, I'll shoot him, so help me God. I'll shoot him for the mean and low varmint he is, anybody that would leave Ben Kelsey after all he's done for you, going sleepless and starving, leading you all without ever a word of complaint!"

She sprang forward, and now she felt her heart beating like a hammer, beating so hard that it rang in her ears and throbbed in her chest until she thought she would burst with the blows. With one hand she reached for Lightning's halter, pulled the horse toward her, the rifle still pointed. "Mr. Hooper!" she shouted. "Take my horse—take him and shoot him. Shoot him! My husband needs food. . . ."

"No, Mrs. Kelsey. We wouldn't take your horse, not Lightning. You wait here. Please, ma'am. We'll find something for Ben. Please, don't distress yourself. Just sit down easy and calm. Just don't take on so, ma'am. Nobody's leavin'. We'll tend him."

Before long she heard a shot. Later they brought her bits of horse meat, roasted lightly, and still later came broth boiled from the bones. It was nighttime before she would stir from Ben's side. He had awakened, and she held the fragrant, steaming cup of broth to his lips.

"Drink it," she whispered over and over again. "You're going to be just fine." She covered him again. She had placed Ma's quilt on top of the other blankets. It made her feel stronger, somehow, to see it.

Ben tried to raise his head. "Whose meat? What horse?"

Nancy shook her head, holding back tears, and she whispered, "I think it's Nick Dawson's horse. Monte."

He sighed. "And my brother? Where's Andy?" If there were other questions in his mind about Andy, he did not ask them. It wasn't in Ben to blame his brother.

"I suppose he went ahead," Nancy said. "Maybe to scout."

"They best go on without me," Ben whispered.

"Hush! Never say that again, Ben Kelsey!" Her tone was severe, more like a mother than a wife.

He slept again, and all night long Nancy sat awake, throwing wood into the fire. Ben would turn and stare at her, then sleep again. Once, staring, he called out through parched lips, "Nancy! Don't leave me."

"I'll never leave you, Ben," she murmured. She bent down and kissed him. "I'll never leave you in this world."

While he slept, she held him, and the night was long, so very long, but there was much to think about, and she did not regret a moment of it. There was a whole lifetime to think about, and loving Ben to think about, and knowing that from now on she would never again have to seek reasons. She would know why she did things, even took risks that seemed downright crazy—she'd know, even without the exact words to explain it. It was all mixed up with loving Ben, with those feelings she'd had alone on the mountain that day, of belonging to the world and everything in it, so that you weren't afraid, but gloried in the chance to find out about life, even the hard parts. It was like John Bidwell had said, that there wasn't any sense in living unless you tried it all. You just had to do the most and grandest thing you could. And if you were a man like Ben, why, you had to go on until your toes touched the Pacific, because nobody you knew had ever done it before.

By next morning Ben was well enough to travel. The men moved with a strange gentleness and walked as if their feet were too large, and some looked down at the ground when Nancy walked past, carrying Lightning's saddle.

Dawson and Bidwell helped Ben to mount. He rode for half a day. Then he got down and walked beside Nancy. "Your darling's feet," he said, but without reproach, "are powerful sore. It's hard enough for him without carrying my weight, too."

He walked close beside her, and their hands touched. He told her, "I was not unconscious yesterday when you picked up that rifle. Although," he added, his lips twitching, "I swear, what I heard you say darn near made me pass out!" He grinned, and his eyes were merrier than Isaac's had ever been. "You, threatening to shoot those men with a rifle! And you meant it," he said, sobering. "I know you meant every word."

"It's true," Nancy said. "I did."

"Charlie Hooper says if California lies beyond those mountains, we'll never make it." He was silent for a time. "But I guess you figure on making it, don't you."

"We'll make it," Nancy said. "I mean to get to California." She turned to grin at him. "You *asking* me, Ben Kelsey?"

"I'm askin' you," he said. "Should have asked you before."

"Well, the answer's the same now as it was then. I'm going

with you, Ben, because I want to. Because"—she dropped her voice to a whisper—"I love you."

"And I," he said, and he took her hand and clasped it tightly in his own, "I wish I knew words better—like Green and the schoolmasters. I've got such—such feelings for you. I wish you could have seen yourself with that rifle, eyes like fire, hair just about standing on end, you were so mad. And your cheeks were fiery red, and you were about the darndest, spunkiest, most..." he stammered, groping for the word, "most *woman* I ever did know. I guess I never thought, Nancy, that you..."

He walked on, and she, smiling softly, nodded. "I know, Ben. I never did think it, either."

That night they heard a pack of coyotes howling, and Nancy awakened from her sleep and saw the mist of clouds lying over the moon, and in her heart was a sudden heaviness, like an omen, a certainty that something was lost. Still half-asleep, she reached for Ben, then for Ann who lay between them under Ma's quilt. They were fine. They were both here beside her. Nancy sighed, then slept again.

In the morning she awakened with that cold, heavy feeling still inside her. Was it Andy? Surely he felt guilty for not speaking up to help Ben. Had he gone off sulking and guilty? He hadn't been seen in three days. Was that the omen? Had he been caught by Indians, and was he dead?

Ben came, carrying the saddle.

"Where's...?" And then Nancy knew. For several weeks now they had not hobbled Lightning, and always in the morning he had been nearby.

"Maybe he wandered on up to that bluff," Ben said, but he avoided Nancy's eyes, and she only nodded, pretending it might be so.

They reached the bluff before the others, and they gazed out over the countryside. Below them lay a valley covered with young, green grass, and at its farther sides rose tall willow trees, sure indications of a water course.

Hooper, following close behind them, took long strides, saying, "I've seen signs of deer. Down in that valley..." He pointed and soon disappeared ahead of them, and then they heard his voice echoing back. "Oh—my God."

"What is it, Hooper?" Ben shouted, his hand cupped to his mouth. He whirled around, looking at Nancy, and he started to tell her, "Nancy, don't..."

But she shook her head and wordlessly began picking her way down the bluff, moving faster and faster down the incline. Ann, braced on her hip, began to squeal and laugh from the jogging motion, until Ben took her from Nancy and put his other arm around Nancy's shoulder. Thus, together they came upon the abandoned camp where Indians had sat in the night by their fires, roasting horse meat.

"Nancy, come away," Ben said. He held her close against his chest, but she had already seen the frame of sapling poles, and stretched upon it, the brown and white hide of a pinto pony.

For a moment Nancy saw a crashing white light, like the sudden momentary blindness that comes from staring too long at the sun. The sour taste rose to her mouth, and the heavy, sick pounding was in her chest, so that she could not speak.

"Nancy, oh, Nancy," Ben whispered, holding her, patting her shoulder in his gentle, awkward way.

She half pulled away from him, and for a moment it seemed her legs would buckle, and she would slip to the ground.

But she took a deep, deep breath. She made herself speak, "I—I never had a horse so keen," she said.

"I know," Ben murmured. "I know."

"The night you were sick, he stayed right by me," Nancy said. Her voice was firm now and clear. "It was as if he knew. He'd bob his head up and down..."

"I know, Nancy, how you set store by that horse." In Ben's eyes was such tenderness that for a moment Nancy had to look away. She did not want to cry. There were still mountains ahead, and a further trail to break.

Ben touched her arm. "Let's carry Ann between us," he whispered.

For a long moment they looked into each other's eyes. A thought passed between them without words; they had each other, and they had Ann. Whatever else happened, they had this love.

"We'll make a seat with our arms," Ben said, and he showed her how, and Nancy remembered that her folks used to carry her that way when she was very young.

They walked slowly down into the soft, green valley. They made their way with the others along the river and the slim, rustling trees, and soon Nancy felt as if she were moving in a haze. A strange sense of peace flooded over her. She marveled at it, for inside the pain remained, too. It was like a wound, but in spite of it, or beyond it, she could feel a peacefulness.

How could a person be grieving and contented all at the same time? She shook her head, puzzled, and Ben, watching her said softly, "Your hair catches the sun like a blackbird's wing."

She stared at him, amazed, and felt a grin coming over her face. She struggled to hide it. She pursed her lips. "Why, Ben Kelsey, just listen to you trying to sweet-talk me, like a young fellow out courting—the very idea!"

He grinned back at her. "Just like a blackbird's wing," he persisted, folding his arms across his chest, his eyes boldly upon her. "Let's go pick us some of those wild grapes."

They had seen the thick vines, and now they picked the luscious fruit, ripe, juicy, and sweet. Hooper had caught three deer, and they had feasted, and now the grapes and the clear water from the stream quenched their thirst.

Ben lay back, drawing Nancy down to him, while Ann slept beside them on the shawl.

"I know we still have to cross those mountains," he said, "and I know we have to hurry before the snow, and I know there's no trail at all, but somehow it doesn't matter."

Nancy smiled. "I guess those grapes hit you like wine."

"No," Ben said thoughtfully, seriously. "That's not it. I still want to get there. I don't want to die! But, well—I guess it isn't just the getting there that counts. Maybe it's—well, knowing we had the—the—well, you know."

"Yes," she said, "I know."

For three days they stayed in the valley. They rested and they ate. Hooper killed thirteen deer. They feasted on the meat and the wild grapes, and then they prepared themselves to push on over the mountain ahead and whatever further mountains would appear.

They gathered together, Bidwell and Ben at the lead. Nancy recalled that first time at Sapling Grove, when they had made a long column and all strained to hear Fitzpatrick's cry and to see his signal, "Moo-oove out!" Now there was not one wagon, not a single animal, no packs, no goods, only the men with their ragged boots and sunken-eyed faces, and Nancy holding Ann. She remembered how she had wished to move far from any other Kelseys. Now she wished more than anything to know they were still alive.

Andy had been gone nearly a week. Maybe he . . . best not to think about it, Nancy told herself, walking in the rhythm she had learned. It was easier now, without the heat of summer. Her feet were accustomed to the sharp, jagged places. On and on—it seemed like one could just keep moving on forever, forgetting the destination, forgetting even the reason, just moving. . . .

As step followed step, one place seemed just like another, and familiar, too, were the distant leaping shapes of trees and crags that played tricks on her eyes and on her mind, resembling now a mountain goat, now a snake or a wildcat, even a man. A man . . . a man walking in a determined, criss-crossing gait toward them, steadily getting closer . . .

No. What manner of man would be here in this wilderness? No. Injuns always crept up behind or rode in groups yelping and screaming. What manner of man . . . ?

"Nancy!" It was Ben, turning back to come for her, for in her daydreaming delirium she had fallen far behind, eyes cast upon the figure that could be a tree or a rock or . . .

"It's a man! A white man! Nancy, it can only mean . . ."

"Andy?"

His name was called by the foremost scouts, by Hooper and Bidwell, and then Ben ran up to see, pulling Nancy behind him, and the two brothers clasped each other, shouting their joy.

"Andy!"

"Ben! Oh, God, I never thought . . ."

In one breath, it seemed, the questions were asked and answered, and all was known. Dr. Marsh's ranch lay just over the hillock. They didn't have to cross that mountain! They were already here.

"This is California?"

"Yup!" Andy, beaming, nodded. "I've already been to the ranch! Come on. We're here! We're already here!"

Nancy stood up as tall as she could, on tiptoe, and she gazed about, wiping her eyes as if to clear a haze.

"And the oranges?" she asked. "And the ocean?"

"You won't see the ocean for a while yet," Andy said. "But there's orange trees, sure enough. Come on, Ben."

"Wait." Nancy took her shawl, wrapped Ann, and gave her to Andy. "You hold your niece for a while, and you men just go on there and sit a spell. I'm going to prepare myself."

"Nancy! We're nearly there," Ben cried. "Have you gone plumb crazy?"

"I'm going to wash myself in this river," Nancy said firmly, "and maybe I'll even wash my hair, so you all just better make your minds up to set there and wait. I don't aim to go down into California looking like a wild Injun squaw."

"Nancy," Ben began, then helplessly he shrugged and pulled Andy away. "Know better'n to back-talk a woman when she gets that way," he muttered, but then he turned again to grin at her.

She stifled a smile and said sternly, "Go on!"

The water was icy cold, and with no soap, she used the stiff leaves of the saplings that grew there, scrubbing herself all over, even her hair, lying back to let the water ooze clear onto her scalp, until she tingled all over from the cold and the clean of it, and felt herself glowing.

When she was dressed again, having vigorously shaken out her clothes, Nancy took the tiny piece of comb she had saved in her pocket and carefully combed through her hair, then braided it fresh and let the long, thick plait hang down her back.

"Now," she called, her eyes gleaming, "I'm ready."

They hurried in the tracks of the others, down, down the last hill, and from there they could see the large, long adobe buildings set before them. In the yards the cattle grazed and pigs rooted, and at the edge of the dwelling stood a grove of trees such as Nancy had never seen before.

The last distance seemed to melt before them. Suddenly they stood beside the doctor, a full-bearded man dressed all in Sunday black, with a clean white shirt and a gold chain for his watch.

Dr. Marsh thrust out his hand, beaming. "Oh, friends! Oh, how I have longed for my countrymen again, companions and neighbors! Make yourselves welcome and at home."

He took Ben aside and told him, "You and your missus must take the bedroom. I have prepared it with fresh skins for your bed."

Nancy made believe she hadn't heard. She kept her eyes down, while inside she felt the delicious excitement at the thought of sleeping in a real bed, *a real bed*, warm and easy.

"We're obliged," Ben murmured, shaking Dr. Marsh's hand, and then he said, "But first there is something I must show Mrs. Kelsey, with your leave."

"Nancy!" He took her arm and led her around the main building to the side, where row upon row of the strange trees grew.

Nancy gazed at them, touched a branch, and fingered the leaves. They were bright green, crisp and shiny. She looked up at Ben. "Orange trees?"

He nodded. "In spring, Andy told me, they're covered with white blossoms and a smell so strong and pretty, why, you think you're in heaven."

"Andy said that?"

"Yup. Guess it's Californ-y makes folks talk that way. He said in summer you can pick the oranges right off the tree and lie back down and squeeze the juice right into your mouth."

Nancy laughed. "Ann will like that!"

"Bet she will."

"But, Ben," Nancy asked, "where's the ocean? Where's the Pacific?"

"Yonder," he said, pointing. "California's a big place, you know."

"There sure is a lot of it," Nancy said, smiling and straining to see as far as she could to distant trees, hills, and canyons.

Ben stood aside to gaze at her, as if they were newly betrothed. "Guess it'll be big enough for you and me," he said, and his eyes sparkled, "and a passel of kids."

"I guess," Nancy said. And hand in hand they walked back to the house.

Epilogue

The Bidwell-Bartleson Expedition of 1841, as it came to be called, was the first wagon train to cross the plains from Missouri all the way to California, and Nancy Kelsey was the first woman ever to make the journey. It is likely that her feat encouraged other women to attempt a similar journey, for the trip was well publicized in Missouri newspapers.

Of the travelers in this venture, many remained in California and lived out their lives as honored pioneers. The most famous was John Bidwell. He became a state senator, a congressman, a candidate for governor (unsuccessful), and was the Prohibition party's presidential candidate in 1892. He was married, became a prosperous rancher in Chico, and died in 1900.

Joseph Chiles became a leader of wagon trains, making the trip three times in all. The last time he brought his children with him. Several places in northern California bear the Chiles name.

Josiah Belden became the first mayor of San Jose.

Charles Weber founded the city of Stockton.

Talbot Green returned to dig up his goods, and ten years later, at a dance in San Francisco, where he was a respected businessman and a candidate for mayor, he was recognized as a thief and an impostor. His real name was Paul Geddes. He was accused of having stolen gold bullion from a Philadelphia bank and deserting his wife and children. He went east to "clear his reputation," but was never heard from again. Green Street in San Francisco was named for him.

Jimmy-John got through the canyon and into California, where he later met many of his friends at Sutter's Fort.

Charles Hooper went east again, returning to California with his family in 1847. He made his home in Napa.

Nick Dawson returned to Arkansas to marry one of his former pupils, then settled in California and lived to the age of eighty-three, the father of many children.

Andrew Kelsey became a property owner, holding the local Indians in virtual slavery. They rebelled and killed him at Clear Lake in 1849.

Nancy and Ben Kelsey traveled widely throughout the west and probably did visit their relatives in Oregon. Ben, in his later years, became a traveling preacher of sorts. He died in 1888.

Nancy lived until 1896, tending her small chicken farm high in the Cuyama Mountains. In that remote community, with no physician nearby, Nancy tended the sick and helped bring babies into the world, riding on horseback where she was needed.

Records do not indicate what happened to the baby, Ann. The Kelseys had several other daughters. One was scalped by Indians during a raid and later died from her wounds.

The Kelseys never became prosperous or famous, but the people who knew Nancy praised her for her kindness and patience. A creek and a small town in California bear the Kelsey name.

Bibliography

★★★

ORIGINAL SOURCES

Belden, Josiah. *1841 California Overland Pioneer, His Memoirs and Early Letters.* Edited by Doyce B. Nunus, Jr. Georgetown, Calif.: Talisman Press, 1962.

Bidwell, John. *A Journey to California, 1841.* Introduction by Francis P. Farquhar. Berkeley, Calif.: The Friends of the Bancroft Library, 1964.

Bidwell, John. *In California Before the Gold Rush.* Foreword by Lindley Bynum. Los Angeles: Ward Ritchie Press, 1948.

Chiles, Col. J. B. *A Visit to California in Early Times.* Berkeley, Calif.: Bancroft Library, 1898 (handwritten).

Dawson, Nicholas. *Narrative of Nicholas "Cheyenne" Dawson.* Introduction by Charles L. Camp. San Francisco: Grabhorn Press, 1933.

De Smet, Father Pierre Jean. *Life and Travels Among the North American Indians.* In *Early Western Travels,* Vol. 28, edited by R. G. Thwaites. Cleveland: 1906.

Hooper, Charles. *A California Pioneer of 1841.* A personal account taken by R. T. Montgomery, Napa, 1871 (typescript). Bancroft Library, Berkeley, Calif.

James John's Journal to California and Oregon 1841 (microfilm of handwritten journal written on the trail). Bancroft Library, Berkeley, Calif.

Kelsey, Nancy. "A California Heroine; The First White Woman Who Crossed the Plains and Sierra." *San Francisco Examiner,* February 5, 1893. Reprinted in "The Grizzly Bear," February, 1937, with comments by Minnie Beatrice Heath.

Williams, Rev. Joseph. *Narrative of Rev. Joseph Williams. The Far West and the Rockies.* Historical Series 1820–1875, Vol. III. Edited by LeRoy R. Hafen. Glendale, Calif.: Arthur H. Clark Co., 1954–1961.

SECONDARY SOURCES

Bancroft, Hubert Howe. *Register of Early California Pioneers.* Baltimore: Regional Publishing Company, 1964.
Benjamin, Marcus. *John Bidwell, Pioneer: A Sketch of His Career.* Washington, 1907.
Eide, Ingvard Henry. *Oregon Trail.* New York: Rand McNally, 1973.
Hunt, Rockwell D. *John Bidwell, Prince of California Pioneers.* Caldwell, Idaho: Caxton Printers, 1942.
Lyman, George D. *John Marsh, Pioneer.* Chautaugua, New York: Chautaugua Press, 1931.
Paden, Irene. *Wake of the Prairie Schooner.* New York: Macmillan Co., 1943.
Royce, C. C. *John Bidwell, Pioneer, Statesman, Philanthropist: A Biographical Sketch.* Chico, 1906.
Stewart, George R. *The California Trail.* New York: McGraw-Hill Book Company, 1962.
Stone, Irving. *Men to Match My Mountains.* New York: Doubleday & Company, 1956, pp. 2–45.
Tunis, Edward. *Frontier Living.* New York: World Publishing Co., 1961.

19